DANNY - DON'T JUMP!
&
THE SHRIEKING FACE

by

HAZEL TOWNSON

Danny– Don't Jump!

Hazel Townson

Illustrated by Amelia Rosato

RED FOX

A Red Fox Book
Published by Random House Children's Books
20 Vauxhall Bridge Road, London SW1V 2SA
A division of Random House UK Ltd

London Melbourne Sydney Auckland
Johannesburg and agencies throughout the world

Danny – Don't Jump first published by Andersen Press 1985
Beaver edition 1987, Red Fox edition 1991
Text © Hazel Townson 1985
Illustrations © Andersen Press 1985

The Shrieking Face first published by Andersen Press 1984
Beaver edition 1986, Red Fox edition 1990
Text © Hazel Townson 1984
Illustrations © Andersen Press 1984

This edition specially produced for School Book Fairs
by Red Fox 1993

Printed and bound in Great Britain by
Cox & Wyman Ltd, Reading, Berkshire

RANDOM HOUSE UK Limited Reg. No. 954009

ISBN 0 09 937501 X

Contents

I

Creation

First there was the business of the cloakroom wash-bowl. All Danny did was to drop a football boot into it, quite accidentally. He never meant to cause a hundred pounds' worth of damage, and privately thought the washbowl must have been faulty to start with. Then there was the newly-planted sapling he walked into when he was seeing what it was like to be blind, and the pile of dirty plates that slid from his monitoring hands halfway through the second sitting of school dinner. (Well, *that* could have happened to anyone, and if folks would go leaving slippery lumps of gristle skidding about in gravy-puddles on every plate, then what could they expect?) But the fact was that by the time Danny broke the headmaster's window—and the Grecian vase that sat on the window-sill—he had already acquired a reputation, deserved or not, as a reckless vandal.

'I fail to understand,' said the headmaster, Mr Cropper, 'how you came to be hurling a Bible across the playground in the first place.'

Danny thought a man in Mr Cropper's position had

no business to fail to understand, especially when Danny himself had just explained that he had been late for assembly, where he was due to read out a psalm, and had slipped on the core of Reg Hopkinson's apple, which wasn't supposed to have been eaten until lunch-time anyway.

Mr Cropper frowned at Danny over his half-spectacles.

'Well, Danny, I must say I'm disappointed in you. I thought you had the makings of a first-rate sensible lad, but just lately you seem to have run completely off the rails. I think it's high time you turned over not so much a new leaf as a whole new plantation. In this school we're aiming for creation, not destruction. Bear that in mind. See if you can't manage to make some positive contribution . . . .'

Mr Cropper rambled on, but Danny had ceased to listen. The word 'creation' had caught on a hook in his mind, and his whole attention was bent on trying to shake it free.

Danny Lyndon really wanted to be liked, and to live up to other people's expectations. To this end he had suffered many things, such as doggedly learning to swim when he hated the water, sharing his crisps when he was ravenous and putting his precious limbs in the paths of lethal cricket balls. All of a sudden, it seemed, he had become unpopular by accident, and he found

that he wanted to set this right. Creation, eh? Some positive contribution? Well, at least he could start by repairing the Grecian vase with his new tube of Super-glue. He would ask for the pieces at once.

'Sir! If you'll let me—!'

'No more excuses, Danny, please. Your ingenuity has already been stretched to the limit.'

'But if you'll just give me . . . .'

'Least said, soonest mended!' Mr Cropper clapped a monstrously heavy hand on to Danny's shoulder. 'Just remember, boy—actions speak louder than words.'

Well, thought Danny, that was true enough; that last slap of the Cropper's had shouted and screamed all the way through Danny's nervous system. The bell's deafening clang now added to the agony and Danny had to go, casting wistful backward glances at the Cropper's wastepaper basket, wherein reposed the shattered ornament.

Never mind; today was Friday. The Cropper went home promptly on Fridays because of his local history meeting, so Danny would sneak back after school and help himself to the broken bits of vase. What a lovely surprise for the Cropper when he got it back good as new on Monday morning!

At four o'clock Danny sneaked back all right, but he had reckoned without Mrs Bodge, who was busy cleaning the headmaster's office.

'What you doin' 'ere, then?' Mrs Bodge instantly smelled a rat. 'Come for a canin', have you? Well, he's gone, so happen it's your lucky day.'

Danny shook his head. 'They're not allowed to cane us any more. They have to forgive us, which is worse. They go on and on and *on*.' Danny proceeded to explain his errand.

'Broke his window and vase with a Bible, eh? Take a real Christian to forgive that!' Mrs Bodge began to chuckle, remembering that Mr Cropper went to yoga classes; he was probably a heathen.

'I *would* like to have a go at mending it.'

Danny edged towards the basket, looking so wistfully woebegone that Mrs Bodge took pity on him. Riffling through the basket, she picked out the vase bits and set them down on the Cropper's desk.

'There you are, then, and I wish you joy of it. Proper jig-saw puzzle that's going to be. Still, I saw one in a museum once, made up from a hundred and eighty pieces, and you'd never have known except it looked as though it was wearing a hairnet.'

'Thanks, Mrs Bodge!' Danny had dropped the pieces—(luckily there were only seven)—into a cast-off envelope from the same basket, and was heading for the door.

'And don't make an 'abit of it!' Mrs Bodge called after him.

At home, Danny spread out his seven pottery pieces on a sheet of newspaper on the kitchen table and carefully unscrewed the top of his Superglue. He began to stir the pieces around into some sort of shape.

'Oooh, that looks interesting! What is it?' asked Mrs Lyndon, who liked to think of herself as a caring mother.

'It's—er—a project. For art.'

'Well, I never! The things they think of at that school! There was none of that in our day, I can tell you! Proper boring old lessons we had. No chance to develop our artistic talents. You don't know how lucky you are!'

'Yes, I do. But don't stand watching, Mum. You'll make me nervous.'

'Go on with you! You're not nervous of *me*!' cried Mrs Lyndon playfully. 'I wouldn't care if I was always nagging you about dropping glue on the table and sticking your fingers together. I *trust* you. Anyway, you haven't told me what it is yet.'

'It's a Grecian vase.'

'Fancy! A sort of kit, is it? Like those pictures they paint by numbers? Well, you make a good job of it, son—(as I'm sure you will)—and you can put it on the mantelpiece in the front room.'

'I can't keep it, Mum. It's for school.'

'Well, surely they'll let you buy it when you've put all that work into it. They used to do that with our sewing and your dad's woodwork. I'll drop a line to Mr Cropper if you like, and ask him.'

'No, Mum!'

Fortunately, Danny's dad came home just then, and Mrs Lyndon bustled off to see to the dinner. Danny heaved a sigh of relief—but it didn't last long. He suddenly discovered that one piece of the vase—a vital bottom bit—was missing. What a rotten shame, just as he'd started to make the whole thing look quite presentable again! You'd think fate would help out a bit when you were trying to make amends. Well, that left Danny two alternatives. He could throw the whole thing into the dustbin and continue his life of shameful notoriety. Or he could go back to school and hunt for the missing piece. Maybe Mrs Bodge would still be there.

Sneaking off quietly, Danny ran all the way back to school, but he did remember to put the top back on his Superglue first.

2

Destruction

Alas! Mrs Bodge and her cronies had gone; that was the first thing Danny discovered. The whole place was locked up and there wasn't a soul about. The second thing he discovered was that the broken pane in the Cropper's window hadn't yet been replaced. The gap was covered with a sheet of thin plywood, which should not be too difficult to remove. In fact, it proved amazingly easy, as though someone had already had a go at it. A few minutes later Danny, feeling like the worst kind of criminal, yet mystifyingly pleased with himself all the same, was standing in the middle of the Cropper's office, having sellotaped the plywood back into place lest some passing nosey-parker should spot the gap.

So far, so good. Now all he had to do was to find the missing bit of vase. He dropped down on to his hands and knees and started a tour of the carpet, peering under desk and chairs, along bottom shelves and round the backs of cupboards. He did not find what he was looking for. Instead, he caught his foot in the telephone flex and dragged the telephone from the desk to the floor with a resounding clang. Immediately a flock of papers rose from the desk like great, white seabirds disturbed from their private cliff. Ominously they swerved and soared and settled all around the room. Danny crouched motionless, shielding his face in horror. Could they have been exam papers, placed in order of merit? Then, suddenly frantic with panic, Danny leapt to his feet and started chasing the bits of paper. One sheet tore as he tried to snatch it from under his foot, and another sheet managed to slip down behind the radiator where no human hand could follow.

It was whilst he was poking about behind the radiator with the Cropper's long, steel paper-knife that he stabbed clean through the lump of 'Plumber's Mate' gunge with which the caretaker had successfully stopped a recent leak. Water began to drip on to the carpet, then to run out at a faster rate, until a sizeable puddle collected.

How cruel Fate could be! From one small good intention the situation had grown into a hideous nightmare wherein Danny, in true nightmare fashion, found his thinking and his action paralysed. He did not know how long he sat there, gazing at the spreading patch of wet which began to lick the edges of more papers. But at last he roused himself and flew off to the kitchen for a mop.

Gone was the moment when Danny might have retreated and given up the struggle to make amends. Now he was so heavily involved in catastrophe that he simply had to put things right. But where was the mop? He had seen a dinner-lady using it that very day, to stem a river of watery custard flowing down the dining-room's centre aisle. But what had she done with that mop afterwards? Danny flung open all the cupboard doors in sight. He even looked in the fridge, reminding himself painfully of his missed meal. At last he remembered the broom-cupboard next to the kitchen door. He opened the broom-cupboard—and a body fell out.

'I can't think what's happened to our Danny,' said Mrs Lyndon, dishing up mounds of mashed potato. 'I never heard him go out, did you?'

'He'll be here as soon as he smells that dinner,' replied Mr Lyndon confidently. 'Never known him miss a meal.'

'If he's gone further than the gate he won't be *able* to smell it.'

'Well, stick his plate back in the oven. I don't see why we should wait. He knows the meal-times and he has a perfectly good watch.'

'It will all dry up in the oven.'

'Teach him the value of punctuality, then, won't it?'

Mrs Lyndon sighed. 'Here, you start your dinner,

then. I'll just give him a shout.'

She went to the front door and called her son's name. There being no reply, she walked down the path to the gate, then called again.

Esmée Bates, who was swinging on next door's gate, said: 'Your Danny's gone back to school.'

'At this time? Whatever for?'

Esmée shrugged and continued swinging.

'He went up School Lane. Nothing else up there that I know of.' Esmée was not quite as unobservant as she looked, though twice as cheeky.

'Well, if you see him, tell him his dinner's ready.'

Mrs Lyndon was not alarmed. She was even trying hard not to be annoyed. Perhaps Danny had forgotten something? A bit of his project, maybe? If he had gone back to school, no possible harm could come to him there. In fact, it was quite heartening, really, to think the lad was so keen on the place.

Having left school early that Friday, Mr Cropper drove first to the barber's, then home for his evening meal. After watching the teatime news on television, he showered and changed, then started packing his briefcase with the papers he needed for the local history meeting. It was his turn to speak tonight, and he had prepared a talk about Keevan Tower, a crumbling local monument about whose origin there was a deal of controversy. The name 'Keevan' was supposed to be a corruption of the French 'Qui vient?' (Who's coming?) but it was Mr Cropper's belief that this Tower had been built, not by the Normans as a Watch Tower, but in 1720 by a gentleman called Sir Cuthbert Keevayne, as a pseudo-Norman folly. Tonight, Mr Cropper intended to spring this information as a surprise upon his colleagues. For evidence, he had made a pile of copies of an ancient plan of the Tower with a quotation underneath it, referring to 'ye incredyble follye of Sir Cuthbt. Keevayne'. He had come across this evidence in an ancient volume dredged up from the back room of the local library, and since the librarian had told him nobody had even looked at the book for eighty years, he felt sure that his information would drop like a bombshell. In fact, the Cropper was hoping to make a bit of a name for himself as a local history researcher.

He stretched out a hand across the dressing-table to gather up this vital pile of copies—and encountered an empty space. He had left the dratted things at school!

'Serves you right for using the school photocopier for your private business,' sniffed his wife.

Mr Cropper looked at his watch. 'Never mind; I'll nip in and get them. Where are my school keys?' He calculated that there was half an hour before his meeting was due to start. Just enough time for the run to school, plus all the fiddle of unlocking and re-locking

the building. No time to waste, however. Mr Cropper jumped into his car, having aimed a brief farewell peck at his wife's cheek, and set off at once.

He had not gone more than a couple of hundred metres when he was flagged down by the vicar, who had just set out on foot for the local history meeting. (The vicar himself could not afford to run a car, but had been secretary of the Local History Society for more years than anyone could remember.)

There was no help for it; Mr Cropper would have to offer the vicar a lift. He pulled up, forced a smile on to his face and flung open the passenger door.

''Evening, vicar!'

'Well met, Mr Cropper!' The vicar was beaming all over his face.

'Spot of business.to do at school first, I'm afraid. Won't take a minute, though. Hope you won't mind waiting in the car whilst I just dash in and out.'

The vicar said he didn't mind at all, and began settling himself comfortably into his seat, just as Danny Lyndon opened the cupboard door and the body fell out.

3
Co-operation

The 'body' rolled over and sat up. It turned out to be notorious trouble-maker Connie Kellow from the top juniors—(a year ahead of Danny). Connie looked far more angry than dead.

'What—what are you doing here?' breathed Danny, considerably shaken.

'I could ask you the same thing. Proper put the wind up me you did, charging round school at this time of night.'

'I thought you were a blooming corpse.'

'I was hiding from you, if you must know. I thought you were the Cropper.'

'Did you get locked in, or what?'

'Sort of.' Connie eyed Danny warily, wondering how far she could trust him. Not far, she decided. Anybody who came to school in polished shoes and clean shirt, paid his dinner-money first thing Monday morning and never missed assembly must be on Their side. However, when Danny began explaining his own movements, beginning with the morning's Bible mishap, Connie remembered Danny Lyndon's new repu-

tation. Perhaps the lad could be trusted after all . . . up to a point. Especially if Connie could involve him in her own plans, so that he wouldn't ever be able to tell tales. Now, there was an idea!

'Like school, do you?' Connie probed. 'One of these keen types, are you?'

'It's all right.'

'You wouldn't be sorry, though, if a meteor hit it or something, would you?'

Danny shrugged. 'We'd only get sent somewhere else.'

'There's nowhere else round here to send us, now they've closed Norton Lane Primary because of the numbers going down.'

'They'd think of somewhere, don't you worry. They'd put a tent up in the park, or something.'

'Well, that'd make a nice change, at any rate. You ever been to a fire?'

'A bonfire?'

'A building on fire, stupid! A bit of real excitement, that is. Just imagine, great crackling flames and thick black smoke and everybody running about with hoses and stuff, and shouting fit to bust. Have you ever seen one close to?'

Danny's imagination made a different set of connections. Hoses—water—that leak in the Cropper's office! For a moment he'd forgotten all about it!

'Hey, you don't know where the mop is, do you?'

'Yeah, it was digging me in the ribs a minute ago.' Connie tipped her head towards the cupboard she'd just fallen out of. 'But what do you want a mop for? Going to be sick, are you?'

'There's a bit of a crisis on. Grab that bucket, will you, and come and give us a hand?'

Danny seized the mop thankfully and set off up the corridor with it, calling back a garbled explanation as he went. Connie could hardly believe her ears. 'You don't mean there's water all over the place? Oh, flipping heck, everything'll be all damp and soggy.' Connie snatched the king-size box of matches from the waistband of her skirt and hurled it into the broom-cupboard in disgust. Then she picked up the bucket and trailed sulkily after Danny.

Meantime, on a park bench a mile away from school, two furtive-looking characters were holding a guarded conversation.

'This had better be good,' said Biffer Bond. 'I was supposed to be going to see my auntie in hospital, and she's due to leave me all her money.'

'Urgent, I said it was; not good. We've nearly been rumbled.'

'Eh?' Biffer jerked back on the seat as if he had just been given a massive electric shock. 'How come?'

'I was in this pub last night, and this guy called Cropper was rabbiting on to his pal about some boring old local history society,' explained Archie Pell. 'I wasn't really listening, just sort of daydreaming over my pint, when all of a sudden I heard the name Keevan. So of course my ears pricked up and I started taking notice. It seemed there'd been an argument about the history of Keevan Tower, and this Cropper chap, who turned out to be a teacher, had gone to the library and got them to unearth a book from some back room or other, all about Keevan Tower. It's stuff they don't put out on the library shelves, 'cause there's only one copy and it's precious, being local history.'

'Blimey, they don't know *how* precious!'

'Well, this Cropper borrows the book, he says, and finds a load of stuff in it about who built the Tower and how it looked when it was first finished. You're getting my drift, are you?'

Biffer certainly was. He gave an agonised but silent nod.

'Cropper decided to take the book to school today and photocopy the bits he wanted, and although he hadn't realised it, one of those bits he was pointing out showed—wait for it!—a plan of the secret underground passage.'

'But you said nobody knew about that passage. You said after they'd blocked one end up, two hundred

27

years ago, nobody ever went near it again . . . .'

'I know what I said. I was wrong, then, wasn't I?'

'Well, what are we going to *do*?'

'Just let me finish my tale before you go completely bonkers. I followed this Cropper home, didn't I, and hid myself in his privet till the lights went out. Then I tried to break in, but no joy. That house is a lot better guarded than a lion's dinner. Everything locked and bolted, even the bathroom windows. All double-glazed as well, so it was no use hurling bricks. In the end I decided to wait until today and catch him at school.'

'That was a bit of a risk, Archie. Suppose he hadn't of . . . ?'

'Well, he did. And me, I just strolled into school as bold as a bailiff and asked my way to the headmaster's office. (That's who this Cropper had turned out to be, see?) I knew he wasn't there, because I'd just seen him talking to the caretaker in the yard. Sure enough, there on his desk was this book, on top of the pile of copies he'd just made. In and out in two seconds, I was, and here they are in this suitcase, safe and sound. Now we'll have a nice little bonfire, and all will be well again.'

Biffer sagged with relief. 'Great work, Archie. You did a good job there! But let's have a look at that book before you set fire to it. Sounds interesting.'

'I only hope there's no more copies of it left.' Archie handed over a fast-disintegrating volume with the back

completely loose, and Biffer began riffling the pages. 'Yeah—that passage is marked, like you said! That was a narrow squeak, and no mistake!'

'That was the very bit he was copying, as well. He's marked the page. See here . . . ?' Archie's voice suddenly faded as he held out the top sheet of the pile on his lap. He had been stricken dumb with horror. For the drawing on the sheet was not Keevan Tower at all, but some simple geometry problem with a triangle ABC inside a circle O, and all that nonsense.

'What's up?'

Archie groaned. 'I only picked up the wrong pile of papers, didn't I?'

'Well, of all the . . . .'

'How did I know the old fool was going to put his book down on top of the wrong pile?'

'You could have *looked*.'

'Don't you dare say a word! Or *I* shall start by asking where *you* were when I was lying in the prickly privet half the night and risking my neck in the school, and . . . .'

'All right, all right; I got the message. But I suppose it'll be me that has to go back to the school now to change them papers.'

'Too late! Look at the time! School's closed long since, and he'll have taken the papers home with him. In fact, if we don't get a move on, he'll have set off for his local history meeting as well.' One agonising thought after another fled through Archie's mind. 'We've gotta stop him, Biffer. Come doom or death, we've gotta grab them papers before he starts dishing 'em out to all and sundry.'

'You're telling me!' agreed Biffer, picturing the twenty thousand packets of cigarettes from the hijacked lorry that were neatly piled in that underground passage. If the local history society started poking about down there it would be doom or death all right.

'Well, what are we waiting for? Where does this Cropper geezer live?'

4
Consternation

'I can't understand it,' Mr Lyndon declared. 'What the dickens has our Danny gone back to school for on a Friday night?'

'Maybe he forgot something. He was doing an art project, all bits and pieces. Easy enough to leave one bit behind.'

'Sounds very fishy to me. Didn't it strike you that he can't get back into school at this time of day? There'll be nobody there. You're too easy-going with that lad, letting him wander off just when he feels like it.'

'Oh, go on, blame me! I didn't even know he'd gone. Anyway, he was here when you came in, so you had just as much chance to notice him sneaking off as I had.'

'If it was something genuine he'd have told us. So he must be up to some mischief or other.'

'Why have you started thinking the worst of the lad lately? You don't give him a chance. He's a good lad, our Danny is. Look how he's tidied up and put the top back on his Superglue!'

'Oh yes, he's a good lad all right! That's why we just

had a bill for a new school washbasin, and all those cryptic remarks last parents' evening about trampled trees and shattered dinner plates.'

'They weren't our Danny's fault, any of those things. He told me all about them, and I believed him. They were accidents, pure and simple. Accidents can happen to anybody!'

As she said this, Mrs Lyndon suddenly clapped a hand to her mouth. Suppose Danny had had an accident just now? Suppose he'd slipped and broken his leg, or cut his head open on that nasty wall at the end of the school playground? Or even worse, suppose some kidnapper had waylaid him halfway up School Lane,

which was always deserted on a Friday night? There were some very funny characters about these days.

'Fred, what if he's in trouble? He *has* been away a long time. I think maybe you ought to go and look for him.'

'He *is* in trouble,' Fred retorted grimly.

'No, I mean hurt.' Mrs Lyndon began twisting her hands nervously together. 'You could just have a walk up to school; it wouldn't take you long. In fact, I'll come with you.'

'No; if I have to go I'll go by myself. You stop here in case he comes back. I'll find him—but I warn you, I'll deal with him properly when I do, make no mistake about that. Worrying us out of our wits!' Mr Lyndon began putting his shoes back on and buttoning up his jacket. 'We've put a lot of hard work into bringing that lad up properly. He's not going to spoil it now. A firm hand, that's what he needs while he's going through this funny phase.'

'What funny phase?' Mrs Lyndon was nearly in tears by now. 'I don't know how you can say such things! He could be lying hurt somewhere . . . .'

'And if he makes me late for my darts match, he'll be in double trouble.'

'Fred—!' called Mrs Lyndon helplessly as her husband strode off at a cracking pace. She ran up the garden path, hoping to smooth him down before it was too late. 'Don't go off in such a fury! You'll only regret it!' But Fred was already turning the corner at the top of the road.

Esmée Bates, still swinging on next door's gate, looked on with interest. 'Hey, are you and Mr Lyndon going to get divorced?' she asked with relish.

'What a blooming mess!' Connie Kellow stared enviously at the ruin of the Cropper's office. She felt quite jealous that a soft-looking lad like Danny Lyndon could have achieved nearly as much destruction in a few careless moments as Connie herself had been planning and dreaming of for weeks.

'Well, don't just stand there! Help me mop up.'

Danny was already on his knees, soaking up water as fast with his trouser-legs as with the mop. Now that he was no longer alone, Danny's panic had subsided and in fact he was beginning to experience a fine clear-headedness he had never known he possessed. Certain facts had fallen neatly into place. Connie Kellow, as well as Danny, must have climbed in through that boarded-up window, and Connie was obviously up to no good. Danny had practically caught her red-handed at something or other. Danny was beginning to feel the stirrings of power.

'How about picking those papers up and spreading them out to dry on the window-sill?'

Connie glanced up, ready with a cheeky retort, then changed her mind and did as Danny suggested. If she helped him, he'd be all the more likely to help her later on. And you never knew, if he turned out to be not quite as soft as she'd thought they might even make a team.

It was whilst Connie was dealing with the papers that she happened to glance up through the remaining window-pane—and spotted the Cropper's car turning into the far end of School Lane!

Connie said several unprintable words, two of which Danny had never heard before, then she grabbed Danny's arm and started dragging him towards the door.

'It's him! Can't let *him* in now!' ('Rotten spoilsport,' Connie was thinking, 'turning up here before I've even had a go!')

'Who—the Cropper? We're done for, then. He's got keys, so how can we keep him out?'

'We'll have to barricade the front door.'

'What with?' demanded Danny reasonably as Connie pulled him along the corridor.

'There's that big, heavy table in the entrance hall, and that great bronze bust of the idiot who opened the school. Then there's the P.E. benches, and the stuff from the office—typewriters and that . . . .'

'We'll never do it in time?' Yet Danny was even

more anxious than Connie to keep the Cropper out. He summoned up every last bit of his energy as the two of them began heaving at the great oak table. It was lucky for them that the Cropper had to fiddle with the padlock on the gate—(which both children had, of course, climbed over)—for this took up another precious few minutes, by which time the barricade was mounted. Connie Kellow had certainly proved herself as tough as any boy.

'There are all the other doors as well,' panted Danny, but Connie reminded him that all the other doors were bolted on the inside; only the front door could be opened with keys. That was a relief of sorts, but Danny immediately began to worry that the front-door barricade would never hold.

'Yeah, 'course it'll hold against a weedy old stick like the Cropper. Don't know what we'll do if he fetches the Law, though. A couple of burly constables would soon shift it.'

Danny hadn't thought of that. He didn't fancy the idea of the Law at all. In fact, it filled him with fresh panic. How had he got into this mess? Up to now, he had been a law-abiding citizen with a grudging respect for authority. He could just imagine his dad's reaction if asked to turn up at some police station to bail out his only son.

'Can't we undo the bolts and nip out the back?'

'Not likely! The Cropper would be sure to see us if we ran off now.'

'Well, let's get back in the broom-cupboard.'

'What, both of us? You must be joking! I nearly suffocated in there on my own. Besides, he'll know we're here because of the barricade, so if he gets in he'll look everwhere till he finds us, broom-cupboard and all.'

Danny turned pale, and for a moment he thought he really was going to be sick. What a final indignity, in front of Connie Kellow!

'Tell you what, though,' Connie suddenly suggested: 'We could get up on to the roof through that trap-door in the cloakroom ceiling.'

This was not such a wild suggestion as it might have seemed, for the school roof was flat, and Connie had often sneaked up there for an illicit spot of sunbathing in the summer holidays.

'The Cropper would see us on the roof all right.'

'Not him! There's that great big ledge all round. We could easy duck down behind that and wait till he'd gone.'

It was worth a try. They could already hear the Cropper rattling at the door and cursing in a most un-headmaster-like fashion. He must already have realised what had happened.

The two of them charged along to the cloakroom,

where they knew that the caretaker's ladder lay neatly along the floor behind the heating pipes. It was tied to those pipes with ropes, and every child was forbidden to touch that ladder on pain of instant expulsion. In no time, Connie and Danny had the knots untied and the ladder set up, though there was one heart-stopping moment when the rising ladder demolished the cloak-room light-bulb with a sound sufficient to rouse the Pharaohs.

'I'll go first,' offered Danny, more out of fear than bravery. He didn't like heights, and had once had to turn shamefully back when halfway up a lighthouse's spiral stair. He must tackle that ladder now, at once, before he had time to think. And indeed, it turned out to be surprising what you could do when death and destruction seemed to be battering at the door. Danny shot up that ladder like the temperature of an Eskimo newly arrived at the equator.

'Watch what you're doing, you nutcase!' Connie yelled as the ladder jumped and shuddered. She threw her weight against the bottom, to hold it steady, but as Danny leapt frenziedly from the top step to the safety of the upper floor, the ladder swung outwards under his final kick, then fell away in splendid slow motion, hanging for a moment in mid-air, completely unsupported, before it fell with a crash right on top of Connie Kellow.

5

Distraction

'Yes?' frowned Mrs Cropper, answering the urgently-ringing doorbell. There were two very odd-looking men on the doorstep, and her first thought was that they had come to offer to clean the drains.

'Is Mr Cropper in? We have to see him urgent,' Archie Pell announced.

'Oh—you've just missed him, actually. He's gone off to his local history society meeting.'

Mrs Cropper was about to shut the door again, but Biffer Bond had slipped his foot into the gap. 'Now, that's a pity. We'll have to go and catch him up. Where would this meeting be?'

By now Mrs Cropper had decided that she didn't like the look of these two at all. They might be planning to mug her husband, or something even worse. So she lied with commendable presence of mind—(as indeed she did whenever an irate parent turned up on the doorstep)—'I don't know where he is tonight. They choose a different meeting place every week.'

'I wonder why they do that?' Archie began to think this local history society might not be as innocent as it

seemed. He took a thoughtful step forward as he spoke, and Mrs Cropper, in turn, retreated a step away from him. Before she realised what had happened, the two men were in the hall and the front door had closed behind them.

'There's no need to be nervous,' smiled Archie like a hungry crocodile. 'All we want to do is to join the local history society.'

'Yeah, we're great joiners, we are,' Biffer agreed, enthusiastically sawing the air with his heavily be-ringed right hand.

'Tell you what, if you can find us the telephone

number of the meeting-place as well as the address, we'll just have a quick word with your husband and tell him we're coming along, seeing we've left it so late. Don't want them to start without us.'

'I've *told* you, I know nothing about the meeting-place. And now, if you'll excuse me, I have a huge pile of ironing to get through whilst my husband is out.'

'Just a minute, lady! I don't think you realise how important this meeting is to us. Could be a matter of life and *death*.' Mrs Cropper did not like the way Biffer suddenly began flexing his knuckles. Wild ideas shot through her brain like a speeded-up film.

'Oh—I'll tell you what! I've just had a brainwave! His diary! He might have written the meeting-place down in there. He's very careful and methodical, you know. He writes everything down. .I'll—I'll go and fetch it.'

'I'll come and help you,' Archie offered genially, taking another few steps forward. 'Don't want you to waste too much of your ironing time.'

'It's—probably in the kitchen drawer.' Mrs Cropper had some hysterical notion of being able to grab the carving-knife for self-defence—but there was no chance of that with Archie Pell breathing down her neck. Archie followed her closely from table to dresser, and there were sounds of drawers opening and shutting smartly. Of course, the diary was not there; never had been there. (As a matter of fact, Mr Cropper did not even keep a diary, dismissing them as 'schoolboy nonsense'.) They tried the living-room next, then the sitting-room, then Mr Cropper's tiny study which was really supposed to be a breakfast-room. There, at last, Mrs Cropper managed to steal a furtive glance at the clock and was thankful to see how much time had passed since her husband left home. Much more than half an hour. Mr Cropper would be safely at his meeting by now, surrounded by stalwart comrades. Thank goodness! Mrs Cropper had played for time and won. Now she could try a fresh manoeuvre.

'Silly me!' she giggled. 'I've just remembered—the meeting's at school tonight. I can't think how I came to forget! You know where the school is, I'm sure—at the top of School Lane?'

'We know!' Archie assured her disgustedly. Biffer was already making for the door.

Trembling all over, Danny Lyndon peered dizzily down from the trap-door. Was Connie dead? She was lying very still, eyes closed and a trickle of blood starting brightly across her forehead. The fallen ladder lay diagonally across Connie's stomach like a giant crossing-out. Obviously Connie needed instant help, but since the ladder had gone, Danny was trapped up there. Fat lot of help he could be! On top of the guilt

43

and horror, Danny almost wept with frustration. Things went on getting worse and worse. The Cropper's leaking radiator was a Bank Holiday treat, compared to this. Now, Danny was faced with an emergency to end all emergencies—a '999' job, an honest-to-goodness matter of life and death. Whatever state the Cropper's room was in, whatever trouble lay ahead, Danny would have to shout to the head for help. Danny wondered what would happen to him. A long spell in Borstal, maybe. Well, even that was better than dragging through life with the death of Connie Kellow on his conscience. Blooming marvellous, though! You started out trying to create and make a positive contribution, and you finished up in the middle of a life of crime!

It was no use shouting from the rafters, Danny decided; no one could possibly hear him from there. He would have to venture out on to the roof all on his own. Gingerly, he progressed across the insubstantial floor and began struggling with the bolts on the little door. Finally he got the door open and emerged on to the school's flat roof. But one step more was all he took. Immediately, the lurching sky and swaying chimneys set his stomach churning. He closed his eyes and clung to the door behind him. In his imagination he had already turned giddy and hurtled from the low parapet to the ground below, where he lay splashed like a tomato on a tax-collector's windscreen. But the memory of poor Connie surfaced slowly, and Danny pulled himself together. He opened his eyes again, lowering his gaze to something more solid. That was when he caught sight of the precarious cat-walk round the edge of the roof—nothing more than rotting wooden slats with goodness knew what hazards down between them if your foot should chance to slip. How could he ever dare to walk on those? All the same, something must be done. He took a deep breath, then removed one hand from the door behind him. Next he took one trembling step forward before closing his eyes again. At last, still metres from the edge of the roof, he managed to make some sort of unintelligible croak which he hoped the Cropper would identify as a call for help. But the croak was carried away on the wind. The Cropper, busy battering at the front door with a rapidly-bruising shoulder, did not hear. In any case, he had just decided to go back to his car and consult the vicar.

'Can't get into the school!' Mr Cropper massaged his wounded shoulder. 'Someone's barricaded the door. What the dickens do you make of that?'

'Very odd,' replied the vicar. 'Are you *sure* you can't get in?'

'How could I not be sure? I've been battering the door—and myself—for the last ten minutes. I wouldn't be surprised if I've done myself a permanent injury.'

'Perhaps the lock's jammed. It happens sometimes.'

'Rubbish! Both keys turned, the latch and the mortice, but I couldn't budge the door itself. Either the caretaker's gone mad, or some of the kids are in there, up to no good.'

'Oh, I can't imagine—!'

'Well, I can! If you knew what some of those kids get up to, vicar, you'd be trying to slip your sermons into the *Jackanory* programme. Why, only today, one of 'em flung a Bible through my window.'

'Dear, dear!' The vicar looked shocked. 'What will you do, then?'

'I shall ring the police, that's what. Your phone's probably the nearest. Do you mind . . . ?'

'Don't you think that's a little drastic, fetching the police to such young children?'

'It's a little drastic for me to be shut out of my school! Drastic, and extremely inconvenient. As it is we shall be late for our meeting—if we get there at all!'

'We could come back after the meeting.'

'And find the place vandalised from top to bottom? Fish-tanks overturned, desks upended, rude writing on all the blackboards? No, thank you! Anyway, I want my sheets of paper.'

The Cropper jumped sulkily back into his car, and slammed the door so hard that the handle fell off on the outside.

Halfway down School Lane, Mr Cropper met Mr Lyndon hurrying along on foot. He braked immediately and wound down his window, recognising a conscientious parent when he saw one, for Mr Lyndon never missed a parents' evening or school function, and had once stood in as emergency referee for a football match when half the staff were down with 'flu.

'Anything wrong, Mr Lyndon?' Two and two were already hurling themselves triumphantly together in Mr Cropper's mind.

'Have you got my lad there?' Mr Lyndon tried to peer into the car.

'Danny? Why, no, not at this time of night. Hasn't he been home?'

'In once, then out again. Came back to school. He was seen.'

'Ah! Well, in that case—' Mr Cropper was interrupted by Mrs Lyndon, who now came panting along behind her husband in a state of terrible agitation. Arms waving wildly, she was shouting: 'Get him down! Get him down before he kills himself!'

Sensing tragedy, the vicar leapt out of his side of the car. He and the others stared first at Mrs Lyndon, then at the spot she was pointing to. There, on the roof of the school, they saw the top half of the figure of a small boy, slowly approaching the edge.

'Danny—don't jump!' yelled Mrs Lyndon frantical-

ly. Then she broke free from the vicar's restraining arm and chased on towards the school.

6

Conflagration

Soon after Danny had gone, Mrs Bodge had discovered the missing piece of Grecian vase in a geranium-pot which had shared the fateful window-sill. She slipped the fragment into her apron pocket, thinking she might call at Danny's house with it on her way home. He'd been so keen to mend that ornament, bless him! The only snag was, Mrs Bodge didn't know where Danny lived.

'Bound to be some of our kids around, though; I'll ask one of them.'

In fact, Mrs Bodge was sent off—(accidentally or on purpose, she never found out which)—in the wrong direction by a lad called Reg Hopkinson, and it was quite a long time before she decided to give up and go home. Only then, when she was halfway back home, did she come across Esmée Bates, swinging dizzily on a gate.

'Danny Lyndon? Yeah, he lives next door, but he's not in. There's nobody in.'

'Never mind, love; you can give this to Danny for me when he comes back.' Mrs Bodge held out the bit of pottery, but Esmée made no move to take it.

'He isn't coming back. He's run away from home and he's hiding in school. His mum and dad are going to get divorced.'

Good-hearted Mrs Bodge was shocked. 'Oooh, what a terrible thing! I don't know what the world's coming to, honest I don't!' She slipped the bit of pottery back into her pocket and went off in the direction of school, tutting and shaking her head. 'No wonder he threw his Bible, the poor lamb!' Well, the least she could do was to go and see if Danny was all right. Had he had a meal? Where was he going to sleep? And what sort of a state was he in? Why, the lad could do anything if he was that upset! Mrs Bodge discovered that she had quite a soft spot for Danny Lyndon, and quickened her pace.

By the time Mrs Bodge arrived at the school gate, the drama was in full swing, Mrs Lyndon weeping wildly in the vicar's arms, Mr Lyndon halfway up a drainpipe trying to reach the school roof, and Mr Cropper speeding off in his car to summon help.

'Well, I never!' cried Mrs Bodge indignantly to the vicar. 'You, of all people, mixed up in a divorce!'

'I beg your pardon?'

'Right under his nose, too, the poor lamb! Where is he?'

'On—on the r-roof!' sobbed Mrs Lyndon. 'He's

going to jump!'

'I'm not surprised!' Mrs Bodge would have said a great deal more, but at that moment there was a blood-curdling yell from the direction of the school and a sickening thump as Mr Lyndon fell from the drainpipe to the playground. Mrs Bodge could not help a small smile of relief. 'Oh, him! For a minute I thought you meant *Danny* was going to jump!'

Mrs Lyndon and the vicar ran to help up Mr Lyndon, who was not badly hurt. He had grazed his hands, bumped his nose and bruised himself a bit, but there was no cause for alarm. Except that he had now

realised he would not be able to reach his son by way of the drainpipe. That meant he was helpless until Mr Cropper came back with reinforcements.

'Can't we find a ladder, or something?' cried Danny's dad distractedly, dashing off on a fruitless search.

Once Mrs Lyndon was assured her husband was still alive, she returned to the front drive, whence she could keep her son in view and call to him.

'Danny—your dad's all right; he isn't hurt! Hang on a minute, love, we're fetching help. Your dad didn't mind about that hundred pounds, nor the tree and the dinner plates. If he seems a bit cross sometimes, it's just his way. Don't jump, love! Promise Mum you won't jump!'

Danny, who had no intention of jumping, could not make out what his mother was saying. All he knew was that he had been spotted, and he presumed that meant his message about Connie had been received. His knees suddenly felt weak with relief and he sat down, which put him out of sight from the ground.

'He's gone!' screamed Mrs Lyndon, making off round the side of the school. 'He's disappeared! He's going to jump from the other side! Oh, Danny!'

Mrs Bodge, who was beginning to get the hang of things, decided that, as everybody else seemed to be in a flap, she had better take charge of the situation. These three had driven the lad almost to suicide, then lost their nerve. It was up to her, Mrs Bodge, to sort the whole thing out.

Cupping her hands, she called out in her loudest voice: 'Can you hear me, Danny? It's Mrs Bodge, what helped you find them pieces. You'll have noticed there's one missing. Well, I've got it right here in my pocket. You could finish your vase in no time, then think how pleased His Nibs'd be. You don't want to do nothing silly till you've mended that vase, now do you?'

No sign from above, just a nerve-racking silence.

'Well, don't just stand there!' Mrs Bodge nagged the vicar. 'At least you could say a prayer for the lad, or think of a good quotation from the Bible.' She herself drew nearer to the school building, ready to call again, but suddenly became aware of two figures approaching the school. Could this be help? She decided to wait and see.

Archie Pell gave Mrs Bodge a friendly wave as he and Biffer Bond strode purposefully up to her. Was she going to the local history meeting, they asked.

'What, me? You must be joking! Takes me all my time to live one day at once, never mind what's past and done.'

'Well, which room is the meeting in?' asked Biffer.

'No meeting here tonight, that I do know! Though I must say there's plenty of other things going on.'

Whilst this exchange was taking place with Biffer,

Archie had moved up to Mr Cropper's window, which he remembered from his visit earlier in the day. Peering in, he saw the papers Connie had picked up and set to dry on the window-sill. They were the very ones he was looking for—the copies of the plan of Keevan Tower with the secret underground passage clearly marked. He couldn't believe his luck! He pushed at the plywood with a heavy hand, and was even more astonished when it fell easily into the room. Archie leaned in after it.

'Now, there's someone with a bit of sense at last!' cried Mrs Bodge. 'Why didn't I think of that?' She presumed, of course, that Archie was on his way through the window to rescue Danny, and ran up to give instructions: 'Go out of that door, turn left, then left again till you come to the cloakroom. There's a trap-door on to the roof. But be careful what you say; the lad's upset. Coax him, don't bully him.' She was completely flabbergasted when Archie Pell began retreating from the broken window again with his arms full of papers.

The fire-engine came clanging all the way up School Lane, with the Cropper's car following and Esmée Bates and a whole crowd of kids running excitedly behind that. Danny heard the noise and stood up again to see if it really was a fire-engine.

'There he is!' the vicar yelled. 'Now, keep still, Danny my boy, and perhaps if we were to sing a little hymn it would help? What about "All things bright and beautiful"?' In his best Harvest Festival voice, the vicar began to sing, though the sound was completely lost among the sirens and the shouts. Mr and Mrs Lyndon reappeared with more disjointed messages, and the fire-engine swerved to a halt. Immediately a turntable ladder soared into the air, bearing a helmeted fireman up towards the school roof. There was a concerted gasp, then silence. Everybody's head turned upwards.

Yes—no—yes—Danny was safely in the fireman's arms at last! Only then did the tension in the watching crowd relax. Mrs Lyndon broke into sobs and collapsed into her husband's arms, whilst Mrs Bodge was surprised to find two big tears rolling slowly down her cheeks.

'Poor little lamb!' she sniffed to the vicar. 'And after all that, they go and make it up again!'

Wrapped in a blanket, Danny babbled hysterically about some girl lying injured with a ladder on top of her, but when firemen went back on to the roof and down through the trap-door they found no sign of an injured girl. True, there was a ladder, lying where Danny must have let it fall. There was also a quantity of broken glass and a single spot of blood, and in

addition the bolts on the back door were unfastened. But there was no trace of any child but Danny. The firemen concluded that Danny was suffering from shock.

By now, as no mangled bodies were appearing, the crowd of onlookers was beginning to feel disappointed, and in fact one or two had started to drift away, when suddenly Esmée Bates cried joyfully: 'Fire!' Surely enough, there was a thick plume of smoke gliding out through the ventilator in the broom-cupboard next to the school kitchen.

7
Retribution

'Thirty copies he made; I heard him say it, not once but three times over,' Archie Pell told Biffer Bond as they sat in Biffer's lodgings counting the sheets they had rescued from Mr Cropper's office.

'Well, there's only twenty-nine sheets here.'

'We might as well have rescued none as twenty-nine. They can find out about the secret passage just as fast from one copy as from thirty million.' Archie looked exceedingly depressed, but for once in his life Biffer came up with an original idea. 'We could always move the cigarettes,' he said.

'What?' Archie was shocked at first, but slowly a grin began to spread across his face. 'You know, Biffer, I think you've got something there! But where could we move 'em to?'

'What's wrong with here? My landlady's just gone off for a fortnight's holiday. By the time she gets back, we'll have sold the lot—or smoked 'em.' Encouraged by one brainwave, Biffer had another. 'We could hire a van from that garage down the street, and drive up to the Tower first thing in the morning. We could shift 'em all in one journey then.'

'Not till tomorrow morning?'

'Nobody's going to start looking for secret passages at this time of night. It's nearly dark already.'

'Sometimes, Biffer, you amaze me!' Archie slapped his companion heartily on the shoulder, starting off a nasty coughing fit. Biffer doubled up in agony, trying to say something between the gasping, heaving, choking spasms. At last he got it out: 'For Pete's sake— gimme a cigarette!'

'Of all the rotten luck!' sneered Esmée Bates. 'Having a fire-engine right on the spot when your school starts burning down! It never had a chance!' Indeed, the firemen had made short work of the barricade, and the fire in the broom-cupboard, which had been started, they thought, by an exploding box of matches. Mrs Bodge declared that no matches were ever kept in there, which made another mystery to add to the evening's toll.

'Never mind; all's well that ends well,' declared the vicar, but Mr Cropper, making a tour of inspection, was not so sure. Those firemen seemed to have squirted water everywhere, even inside his own room, though it was well removed from the site of the fire. Everything in Mr Cropper's room was damp, and some of his possessions seemed to have been moved about rather a lot. In fact, a few of them were missing, which puzzled him until Mrs Bodge came offering to help, and told him about the two men making off with his papers. (Geometry problems? Who on earth would want those?)

'You know, Mrs Bodge, there have been some funny goings-on at this school tonight, and I don't think we've heard the last of them yet, by any means.'

'But why would anyone want to steal your papers?'

'I don't know yet, but I shall certainly look into it.'

'There's something else you ought to look into, as well. That lad, Danny Lyndon, was ever so upset about your vase. He wanted to find all the bits, so he could glue them together again.'

Mr Cropper looked up sharply. 'Oh, dear! You're not suggesting that was what made him so upset he was going to . . . ?'

'Jump? Well, it might have had something to do with it, but he was really fretting about his mam and dad splitting up.'

'Splitting up? The Lyndons? Why, they're the very last people I would have thought of . . . .' Mr Cropper sat down suddenly. 'This is a night of surprises, and no mistake! So that's why the boy got into his silly phase these last few weeks?'

'Yes, and maybe if you'd all been a bit more understanding, this would never have happened.'

A mile away, in the hospital waiting-room, Mr and Mrs Lyndon sat drinking cups of tea while Danny underwent a check-up. As the boy was still insisting upon his unlikely tale of the dying girl—(his latest version was that she had burnt up in the fire)—there had been some talk of keeping him in overnight, for observation.

'What on earth possessed the lad?' worried Mr Lyndon. 'Rampaging about on the school roof! I can't understand it!'

'I'm sure there's a perfectly simple explanation,' insisted Mrs Lyndon, 'just as there was about the sink and all those other little accidents.'

'In my experience, the word "accident" is often just an excuse for all sorts of unsavoury goings-on.'

'Well, don't forget the boy's ill. We've got to be very gentle with him.'

Mr Lyndon grunted, tenderly massaging his damaged nose and trying to ease his bruises on the hard wooden bench. If anybody was ill, he felt, it was himself, but of course it would be Danny who got all the sympathy.

Presently a nurse appeared and said that Danny could be taken home. 'I should put him straight to bed, though, without discussing this any more. And let him take things easy tomorrow. He's a bit shaken up and confused.'

Thankfully, the Lyndons collected their child and ordered a taxi to take them home. On the way they tried hard to talk cheerfully of anything but the subject on their minds.

'Well, Danny, your mother tells me you're doing a project for art, then.'

'Am I?'

'Of course you are, dear! You've just forgotten, but never mind.'

'Dad, isn't anybody going to look for Connie Kellow? She could be bleeding to death, or anything.'

'Are you still going on about . . . ?'

'Sssh!' Mrs Lyndon laid a warning finger to her lips. 'Get your key out, Dad, we're nearly home.'

Mr Lyndon felt in his pocket for his front door key. It was not there. He had rushed out in such a hurry to look for Danny that he had forgotten to pick it up. Still, he remembered having told his wife to stay at home, in which case he wouldn't have needed a key. So this was all her fault.

'Have you got *your* key?' he asked Mrs Lyndon. But his wife kept her keys in her handbag, and of course you don't give a thought to accessories when you are chasing your missing son. Her handbag was still on the kitchen dresser.

'Are we locked out?' Danny showed a spark of interest. 'I could climb in through the kitchen window. Mum never shuts it properly.'

'You've done enough climbing for one night. Leave it to your dad.' Mrs Lyndon suddenly had another thought: 'Oh, Fred! Haven't you any money for the taxi, either? We'll have to borrow from Mrs Bates then, but I do hate borrowing.' She jumped crossly from the taxi and laid a hand on the Bates's garden gate. It promptly fell apart at the hinges, subsiding to the path with a deafening clatter. (So much for Esmée's swinging marathon!) Mrs Lyndon looked shaken and upset, but Danny said, 'Never mind, Mum! It was only an accident.'

Ten minutes later, when Mr Lyndon was halfway through the kitchen window—(and a very tight squeeze he was finding it to be)—he felt an even tighter grip on his ankle and a stern voice called: 'Now then! Let's have you out of there!'

It was the local police constable, newly drafted here from country parts, and anxious to make a good job of his new assignment.

It took red-faced Mr Lyndon quite a time to extricate himself from the window, whereupon he protested that he'd lived in that house for fourteen years.

'That's what they all say,' smirked the constable, pulling out his notebook and pencil.

'But you surely don't think I'm a burglar? There's a perfectly simple explanation. The whole thing's just a little accident.'

The constable grinned. 'In my experience,' he said, 'the word "accident" is often just an excuse for all sorts of unsavoury goings-on.'

8
Exploration

'I didn't start that fire,' said Connie Kellow, meeting Danny at his gate very early the next morning.

'I never said you did.'

'No, I know.'

'How's your head?' Connie had a plaster on her forehead where she had cut it when the ladder fell.

'Oh, it's okay. How's yours?'

'Nothing wrong with my head.'

'I heard you'd been having visions, seeing dead bodies all over the place.'

'Yeah, I need my eyes testing.' Danny began to walk away, having lost interest in Connie now that he knew she was alive and well, but Connie stopped him. 'Hang about a minute! I've got something to show you. That's why I've come round here.' She began unfolding a grubby sheet of paper which she had fished out from behind the radiator in the Cropper's office the previous night.

'See that? It's a plan of Keevan Tower.'

'So?'

'So it's got a secret underground passage. Bet you

never knew.'

'Bet the builders never knew, either.'

'No, honest! Have a proper look!'

Danny looked. 'Huh!' he said at last.

'Suppose we go and sniff it out? Just you and me. Be a good adventure, that would.'

'No, thanks.'

'Scared, are you?'

'Let's just say I don't want to make a fool of myself, looking for something that isn't here.'

'It *says* it's there. Can't you read?'

'Then how come you're the only one that knows about it?'

Connie's lips tightened. 'Okay then, *be* like that! I can find it by myself.' She stuffed the paper into her pocket and walked away whistling.

'Danny!' Mrs Lyndon, still in her dressing-gown, peeped anxiously round the half-open front door. 'You're up early. Are you all right, love? I was going to bring you your breakfast in bed.'

'I'm fine, Mum!' Danny didn't sound it. Had he just let a perfectly good adventure slip through his fingers?

Mrs Lyndon had been going to ask, 'Was that the girl. . .?' but stopped herself just in time. Best not to start Danny off on his fantasies again. In fact, she must try to keep him occupied all day. 'Tell you what, how about coming shopping with me after breakfast? We could buy a new jig-saw puzzle and I'll help you get it started.'

Connie Kellow, never having tried to live up to anybody's expectations except her own, had no difficulty in reaching Keevan Tower very early that Saturday morning, whilst the dew was still deep enough to soak her socks and track-shoes. It was a cool day with a threat of rain, and there was nobody else about; only a self-drive hire van parked behind the Tower. She stood for a while, studying the plan she had found, and looking at the ruin with a new eye. Then she climbed over a tumbledown bit of wall that said DANGER—KEEP OUT and began carefully searching the ground.

Half an hour later, Connie came across a small hole overgrown with creepers. There was a big flat stone nearby, which looked as if it might once have covered the hole, and the creepers could be coaxed aside to reveal a flight of worn steps leading down into the earth. It was all exactly as the notes had described. Fishing out her torch, Connie started carefully downwards and kept on—until she heard muffled voices. She stopped and listened. The voices seemed to be rising from below. Could the place be haunted? There was also an eerie dragging sound—like heavy boxes being pulled along rough ground.

Well, this was a real adventure, all right! Not only was there a proper secret passage, but there was somebody—or something—actually in it! If only that Danny Lyndon hadn't been so soft, she'd have had somebody to share the fun with. ('Have to put new life into him one of these days,' Connie promised herself.)

Bravely, Connie continued her progress. It took her a few more minutes to realise that the voices and dragging sounds were getting nearer. By the time she actually caught sight of the two men, it was far too late to run away.

Danny Lyndon mooched around his back garden, kicking at bits of stone. He was utterly fed up. Since Connie's departure he had had to endure a series of excruciating scenes. First there was his dad, still smarting from his tangle with the Law, trying hard to 'understand', yet obviously resentful at the unfairness of it all, since nobody had understood *him*. Then there was his mother, treating Danny with exaggerated fuss and false jollity, as if he were royalty about to be wrongly beheaded. Worst of all, the Cropper had turned up whilst breakfast was still on the table, and had actually tried to apologise for misunderstanding everything. He had kept on casting meaningful glances, not only at Danny but at his parents too, provoking puzzlement in Mum and further irritation

in Dad. All sorts of cryptic remarks fell from the Cropper's lips, yet none of them made sense. It was worse than anything Danny had ever lived through, with the possible exception of the thought that he might have killed Connie Kellow. So what with one thing and another, the whole situation at home just now was unbearable. If this was the result of trying to live up to people's expectations, then the sooner Danny stopped, the better. He would abandon all attempts to please the grown-ups and concentrate on his contemporaries instead. Connie Kellow was the only person today who had treated Danny normally. Perhaps if Danny were to follow Connie up to Keevan Tower after all . . . ?

Danny glanced around. His mother was furtively watching him through a looped-up corner of kitchen curtain. She beamed a great, false smile when she saw she was spotted. Danny gave her a half-hearted wave, then ambled carelessly round to the front of the house—where he caught sight of Mrs Bodge, approaching along the street with a huge bunch of flowers!

That did it! Danny broke into the fastest run of his life. It took him no more than fourteen minutes all the way to Keevan Tower.

He was just in time to see two unsavoury-looking men bundling a struggling, protesting Connie Kellow

into a van and driving away. Danny noted the number
of the van and ran straight home again.

'Connie Kellow's just been kidnapped!'

'Danny, where have you *been*? I thought we told you
not to leave the garden today, except with one of us?
You're supposed to be convalescing. And Mrs Bodge
has come to see you. Look at the lovely flowers!'

Danny spun round and ran off again to find a
policeman.

9
Conclusion

On Monday morning, the crowd in the school playground pressed close around its heroine, Connie Kellow. To have been kidnapped by cigarette thieves, then rescued as the thieves were caught, was enough to ensure Connie's glory for the rest of the term. But strangely enough she had turned the focus of attention on to Danny Lyndon.

'As for him, he was scared going up the ladder, and he was scared to look for that underground passage. Left me to catch them cigarette thieves on my own,' she declared, gesturing rudely at Danny who hovered on the edge of the throng.

'Fat lot of good it would have done you if they'd shredded you up for extra tobacco,' Danny pointed out. 'I was the one who set the police after you. If it hadn't been for me . . . .'

'If it hadn't been for you, capering about on the school roof last Friday, the school might have burnt down,' cried Esmée Bates.

'Yeah, trust him to spoil all the fun!'

Danny Lyndon stared at the crowd of faces, turning

now towards him and beginning to look decidedly hostile. 'There's no pleasing some folks!' he said disgustedly. He felt aggrieved that Connie Kellow should be the heroine of the moment, whilst he had had to make do with a series of tickings-off for disobeying various instructions, and being rude to Mrs Bodge. At one point on Saturday, Danny had almost begun to feel that he and Connie had shared an adventure after all; might even share others in the future. But Connie's present betrayal had hurt him badly. She ought to have been grateful for being rescued, but instead of that she'd done her best to belittle his efforts and put him in the wrong.

'You should have seen him at the top of that ladder!' Connie was jeering now. 'I don't know which of them was dithering the most. It could've killed me, that ladder could!'

'Serves you right for breaking into school in the first place!'

'I only went to get my cardigan. Anyway, hark at him! Little Goody Two-Shoes! You know what *he* was up to? He was snooping round the Cropper's desk, looking through all his papers. No wonder he always does so well in the exams!'

'You rotten liar!' Danny Lyndon saw red. He swung his lunch-bag up and lunged at Connie with it. Four salami sandwiches, one banana, one orange and a bag

of Chipples would have made quite an impact on Connie's cheeky face. But unfortunately the lunch-bag flew out of his hand and soared across the playground in a wide, impressive arc. Danny closed his eyes. He knew what was going to happen, and it did. There was an ominous tinkling sound, followed by a more substantial crash.

'That's more like it!' Connie Kellow crowed. 'I knew he had it in him!' She set the whole crowd cheering, and led them in a circular war-dance round Danny. Finally, she leapt to Danny's side, winked, held out her hand and grinned. 'Shake!'

76

All at once, Danny Lyndon realised with amazement that he had achieved his life's ambition. He was popular at last.

The Shrieking Face

That was the moment when Kevin fell out of his tree with a blood-curdling scream, Mum ran to the door to rescue him, and Rosco burst in, leaping excitedly with muddy paws on to the pile of freshly-ironed pillowcases. As Mrs Lang bore in a grazed and loudly-wailing Kevin, Angus decided to flee to his bedroom. On the way, he shouted defiantly from the staircase:

'Anyway, my peace picture was the best, even with you lot in it!'

'And that's enough of your cheek!' retorted Mrs Lang.

The Shrieking Face

Hazel Townson

Illustrated by Tony Ross

Chapter 1

Angus Lang crackled with rage. He plunged his paintbrush into thick black paint then daubed a great, shrieking face across the middle of his picture. It was the face of his teacher, Mrs Crake, with her mouth wide open in a nasty, ugly shout.

'Serve her right if she recognises herself,' thought Angus. For that was just how Mrs Crake looked when she was going on at him all the time, nag, nag, nag!

'Angus Lang, I won't tell you again to stop talking!'

'Angus Lang, you are capable of much better work than this!'

'Angus Lang ... Angus Lang ....'

Slap, slap, the lines on the picture grew thicker, until Angus began to feel really good, as though he had just kicked a vital goal or speared a dragon. He sat back to admire the face, then added, with a final, vicious dab, a great black spot on the end of the nose. Perfect!

The picture was supposed to be called 'Peace'. It was something special they were all doing for a big competition. And in fact, until Mrs Crake had rattled him, Angus had been enjoying his own interpretation of that word ... green countryside,

5

ending in a colourful garden where his dad was digging, his kid brother Kevin was playing with Rosco the dog, and his mum sat knitting in a deck chair. Now this happy scene looked as if it had been gobbled up by Satan himself.

The moment's triumph passed, and reaction set in. Dread crept into Angus's stomach and lay there like a heavy load of stone-cold fish and chips. What would old Corny say when she saw what he'd done? She might tear his painting up, or stand him in a corner, or send him to the Head. But worse that any of these things was the fear of Corny's clever, biting sarcasm which could reduce even a rugby front row forward to the size of a Tom Thumb.

Angus leaned across his painting, circled his arms protectively about it and willed the face to disappear. But of course it didn't, and it was only a matter of time before Mrs Crake loomed up behind him, prised him backwards—and gasped!

There was a moment's silence, during which the whole of Angus's life passed through his drowning mind. Then Mrs Crake said: 'Why, that's wonderful! That's simply wonderful!'

What did she mean? Was this a new sarcastic turn? But no; Mrs Crake was really pleased with the picture. In fact, she seemed almost moved to tears as she tenderly gathered up the wet painting and transferred it to her table.

'Well, Angus Lang, I always said you had it in you. Look, class! This picture says in a few simple lines what the whole Campaign for Nuclear Disarmament has been trying to say for years. There looms the face of the monster which threatens the peace of the world. We all know what that monster is, and how it hangs over everthing we do . . . .' At this point a definite dewy glitter could be detected in Mrs Crake's eye, and it was just as well that the bell went for the end of afternoon school.

Angus ran all the way home, anxious to flee the guilt of having turned old Corny's brain. That must be what he had done. All that rubbish she'd talked about his picture! The only monster Angus had seen hanging over everything he did was Mrs Crake herself. She must have recognised her own face, after all, but to ramble on like that about it! She must have gone completely bonkers. Perhaps she would have to see a psychiatrist. Perhaps she'd have to leave school. Great! Yet at the same time, terrible! For it was all Angus's fault.

When Angus arrived home he found Rosco the dog in disgrace for chewing a sofa cushion, his kid brother Kevin all bandaged up after a fall, and his mother shouting at his dad who had just come home early because the factory was out on strike.

'I don't know what gets into you lot these days! You're always out on strike. It's bad enough trying to manage on a decent week's wages, never mind strike pay . . . .'

'Exactly!' said Angus's dad, giving Angus a wink. 'Anyway, I notice there's always enough money for Mars bars for our Kevin every time he falls over. You're spoiling that lad rotten, and I don't just mean his teeth.'

'Leave him alone. His knee hurts, doesn't it, Kevvy?'

This was the cue for Kevin to start wailing, so Dad, to change the subject, asked Angus what he'd

been doing at school.

'Drawing a picture of peace,' replied Angus shiftily, not wanting to think too hard about the afternoon's events. 'For a competition. There's a prize for the best.'

'Well, you won't win it, never fear!' his mother butted in. 'You're about as artistic as your dad, and the best thing he's ever likely to draw is the old age pension.'

'If I live that long,' retorted Mr Lang. 'Peace, eh? Well, there's not many of us has much idea what that looks like, I can tell you!'

Chapter 2

'Angus Lang! The Headmaster wants to see you.'

Angus in the middle of next day's robust rush to freedom, came to a pale and shaky halt. Retribution at last! Old Corny had obviously come to her senses and complained. Angus trailed slowly back across the playground, wondering what to say.

'I don't know what came over me!' was his grandma's line whenever she had one of her dizzy turns. 'Just an experiment,' was his mother's excuse when the dinner went wrong. ('If I didn't try something new now and then, you'd only say I was stuck in a rut.') Or there was the time his Uncle Ben painted the front door in red, green and yellow stripes, claiming: 'I just felt like it. What's wrong with a bit of self-expression?'

In the end, Angus said none of these things. He didn't have the chance, for the Headmaster, Mr Drabble, did all the talking.

'Well now, Angus, for once you seem to have covered yourself in glory. That's a very fine picture you've done for the competition. So fine, in fact, that we're sending it forward, as this school's one permitted entry, to the regional finals. What have you got to say to that, eh?'

Angus had nothing to say. He was dumbfounded.

'Peace swallowed up by war,' Mr Drabble went on. 'Or the threat of war, which is nearly as bad. You know, my boy, we may have a winner there. It's a very discerning piece of work; almost a stroke of genius. And I must say I'm glad that it's come from you—from a boy who has hitherto been—(let's face it!)—something of a handful. Lazy, dishonest, inattentive, disruptive . . . .'

This was more like it! Finding himself on familiar ground again, Angus perked up. He even managed a rueful grin as he braced himself for the punishment to come. When the Headmaster finally stood up and reached across his desk to shake Angus's hand, the boy almost flinched. Yet all Mr Drabble said was: 'Congratulations! And let this be the first of many triumphs.'

By the time Angus stumbled out into the corridor he felt weaker, sicker and more confused that he usually did after six of the best. He ambled home in a daze, wondering whether he was the one going crazy, and not Mrs Crake. There was certainly something funny happening. Was this what folks felt like in fairy tales when they'd just had a spell put on them?

When he did get home, he found Rosco shut out for gnawing the table-leg, Kevin halfway up a forbidden tree, and his dad setting off with flask

and sandwiches for the night-shift picket line. Inside the house, Mrs Lang was ironing bad-temperedly, muttering away to herself about poverty, slavery and utter selfishness.

'Hi, Mum! What's for tea?'

'Bread and cheese. And you needn't look like that. Think yourself lucky it's not just bread, what with this dratted strike, and the rates and electric gone up again.'

There was more of the same, but Angus closed his ears and moved over to the telly. Might as well watch the children's programmes until the bread and cheese appeared. He turned the switch and settled down hopefully. After a minute, he realised something was wrong, advanced upon the set and gave it a couple of hearty blows on the right-hand side. This usually worked, but not today. Neither sound nor picture was forthcoming.

'Mum, I think the telly's broken.'

'It had better not be!' Mrs Lang laid down her iron and marched towards the set. Twiddling knobs furiously, she berated first the set and then her son, in ever-mounting fury.

'What do you think you're playing at, you great, clumsy . . .?'

'It wasn't me, Mum! I only turned it on.'

'I saw you clouting it on the side. How many times have I told you not to touch that set? If you want it on, you ask me. I'll do the turning.'

'But you were busy ironing . . . .'

'Ironing? Oh, no!'

Mrs Lang leaped back to the ironing board, but it was too late. A great, brown patch had been scorched in the middle of Mr Lang's best shirt.

This was the moment when Kevin fell out of his tree with a blood-curdling scream, Mum ran to the door to rescue him, and Rosco burst in, leaping excitedly with muddy paws on to the pile of freshly-ironed pillowcases. As Mrs Lang bore in a grazed and loudly-wailing Kevin, Angus decided to flee to his

bedroom. On the way, he shouted defiantly from the staircase:

'Anyway, my peace picture was the best, even with you lot in it!'

'And that's enough of your cheek!' retorted Mrs Lang.

Chapter 3

'There is no doubt at all about my choice,' said the Principal of the College of Art. 'Only one of these pictures really has anything to say. The rest of them are insipid, if competently-painted, little day-dreams.'

'Oh, I don't agree!' objected Mrs Moxton, President of the Amateur Landscape Painters' Club. 'Every one of these pictures has a great deal to say. Look at this one, for instance; an old lady feeding the birds in a park full of flowers. Peaceful old age, enjoying the beauties of nature.'

'Sentimental rubbish! An old woman like that would probably have arthritis, inadequate heating, no proper dinner and only the birds for company. Peace my foot! More like a lull between battles.'

'All right then, what about this picnic scene?'

'My dear lady, I ask you, have you ever had a peaceful picnic, with no flies, wasps, wet grass, cow-pats, forgotten hampers, accidents, boredom, bulls, sudden downpours . . . ?'

'Well, we all know life is full of little disappointments, but if you're going to go on like that all the time . . . .'

The chairman of the Regional Selection Panel cleared his throat nervously. 'I think a process of

elimination would be best. Perhaps if we could reduce the number of likely winners to three or four, then take a vote on it . . . .'

There was much more argument, but in the end that was what they did. The Panel members found they were unanimous in disliking at least a dozen pictures. This spurred them on to make further decisions, until in the end only three works of art were left. A final vote was taken, and Angus Lang's picture was declared the regional winner, to go forward to the national finals in London.

'I should just think so!' declared the Principal of the College of Art, who had wasted an afternoon of perfect sketching weather. 'It's a mistake to mix amateur and professional judgements on these occasions.'

'Justice has to be seen to be done,' snapped Mrs Moxton nastily, while the chairman of the Panel dithered about trying to shepherd everyone from the room.

Mr Drabble received the news by telephone within the hour.

'Absolutely delighted to tell you that your school's entry has been chosen.'

The Headmaster danced a little jig about his room. 'What did I say?' he asked himself in the mirror. 'We knew that lad's picture was a winner, didn't we? What an honour for the school! If he wins the national prize, I'll give the whole school a half-day holiday.'

Mr Drabble sent for Angus at once to tell him the glad tidings, but Angus was not in school. Rosco had followed him on to the bus that morning, and Angus had had to take the animal back home. By then he was so late that he dared not face the wrath of Mrs Crake, so he went for a walk by the canal instead, and was actually offered a lift on a barge. Angus knew not to accept lifts from strangers in cars, but no one had ever said anything about barges. The whole thing seemed so tranquil and safe and tempting that he clambered aboard.

The barge was carrying some goods from a local factory to Liverpool, whence they were to be shipped abroad.

'It's a lot cheaper than sending 'em by road,' the bargee told Angus, as he peacefully puffed his pipe. 'Now that everybody's trying to keep their costs down, canals is coming back into their own.' Angus felt that he had now learned more than he would have done in a whole day at school, so he stopped feeling guilty and settled down to enjoy himself. By afternoon, he had come to know the bargee well enough to ask him to write a note, signed 'J. Lang', explaining that Angus had not been feeling very well yesterday, and could his absence please be excused.

'You know, it's a great life this,' said Tom the bargee when the note was finished. 'Nobody to bother you, once you've loaded up. Nice leisurely progress—(See that bird over there? That's a heron that is!)—plenty of fresh air and lovely scenery. What more could you want?'

What, indeed? It was pure escape from all the naggers in the world.

'I wish I'd known how peaceful it was out here,' sighed Angus. 'I could have put you in my picture, heron and all.'

Chapter 4

The great news came through on the breakfast-time bulletin:

'The nationwide children's art competition, organised by PANIC—(the Peace-Among-Nations Inspirational Committee)—has been won by Angus Lang, a pupil of Bordham Primary School. Angus's picture, which has been described as "Quite remarkable!" by Sir Desmond Snubbs, the President of the Royal Academy, will be on view in the Taste Gallery until the end of this month.'

'Turn that noise down!' shouted Angus's mum from the far side of the kitchen, where she was frying bread in fat already speckled brown by yesterday's sausages. 'I can't hear myself think in a morning!'

'Lucky you!' grunted Mr Lang from behind his copy of the *Sun*.

'And where's our Angus? He's going to be late for school, as usual.'

Angus was still in bed, enjoying the tail-end of a dream in which he and Tom, his bargee friend, were sailing along towards a free Amusement Park with a cargo of walnut whips. Angus had managed another lift with Tom yesterday—(twenty miles of glorious canal, then back home on the bus)—other-

wise he would have been in school to receive the advance news of his triumph. As it was, he had no idea what lay in store for him when Rosco finally leapt on to his chest and started to nibble his ear.

Angus rose reluctantly. It would have been nice to take another canal jaunt today, but he knew that Tom was now out of reach until next Friday, when he would pass by on the way to Liverpool once more. School this morning, then. Thinking gloomily ahead, Angus remembered the spelling test that would be coming up straight after prayers. Not only had he forgotten to learn his spellings, but he had also lost the list, so that he could not even steal a quick last-minute glance from inside his hymn-book. Perhaps if he prayed hard instead, he would receive inspiration at the proper time, and even get full marks. Better still, could he force two fingers down his throat and make himself sick? So absorbed was he in these alternatives that he was completely taken aback when his best friend Jeffo, meeting him at the garden gate, slapped him hard on the shoulder and shouted breathlessly, 'Hey, what's it feel like to be famous, then?'

'What are you on about?'

'Oh, come off it! Stop acting modest.'

'Honest, Jeffo, I don't know what you mean.'

The two boys argued at cross purposes all the way to the bus stop, and Angus was still no wiser when the bus arrived. Then what a reception he got! Not only was he man-handled forward to the seat of honour at the front, but the entire bus-load of kids began to sing:

Nice one, Angus, nice one, son!
Nice one, Angus! Let's have another one!

'I think you're all barmy!' he finally managed to groan.

'Hey, he doesn't know! He wasn't in school yesterday.'

'No, he was playing hookey again, the crafty devil.'

'Didn't you even listen to the news this morning, Angus?'

'You've only won that blinking Peace prize, that's all.'

'And got us a holiday next Friday afternoon.'

'And had your picture hung up in a fancy frame in a London gallery.'

Angus's stomach lurched, and he looked around desperately for somewhere to be sick.

'You okay?' asked Jeffo with concern.

'No!'

'But you must be pleased. That prize is five hundred quid and a free trip to London. Boy, what could I do with five hundred quid?'

'My mum'll make me put it in the bank,' said Angus gloomily.

'Well, she'll have to let you have it one day. It might double in interest before then. Anyway, she can't stop you taking the free trip to London.'

'She'll want to go with me,' moaned Angus. 'Look, I'll have to get off the bus and go home.'

'Oh, no you don't! Just take a few deep breaths and you'll be all right. Our whole day depends on you being there. They've got a special assembly planned in your honour, so we'll miss the spelling test for a start. And after that . . . .'

As Jeffo outlined the day, Angus began to feel stranger and stranger, as though he had turned into someone else. All his life he'd been a failure, an infuriating nuisance who brought out the worst in people like his mother and Mrs Crake. How could he suddenly have changed? He remembered the 'magic spell' feeling he'd had before, and thought that it did almost seem like a fairy tale—Frog into Prince, or Woodcutter's Son into King. Angus actually rubbed his eyes and shuddered, as if he felt the magic creeping over him. 'Let's hope it's all going to finish with a "Happy Ever After",' he thought.

Chapter 5

Mr Drabble shuffled the pile of papers in front of him and finally came up with a map. This he handed across his desk to Angus.

'There you are, then. That shows you how to get to the Taste Gallery. I've marked the nearest tube station in red, but of course you can always take a taxi if you're doubtful.'

Angus could not imagine his mother 'wasting good money' on a taxi. On the other hand, he couldn't imagine her on the underground escalators either.

'Couldn't we get the bus, sir?'

Mr Drabble grinned. 'Oh, I wouldn't do that if I were you. They're not like the buses up here, you know, bumbling along and dropping you off obligingly at your own front gate.'

Angus began to look so miserable that Mr Drabble took pity on him.

'Cheer up! You're a celebrity now, you know. What's a little journey across London? Think of all the fuss and glory when you get there, met by Sir Desmond Snubbs himself and I-don't-know-who-else.'

'That's what I am thinking, sir.'

'Angus Lang, I do believe you're scared.'

'Petrified, sir. Honest, I'd rather be one of the angels in the infants' Nativity play.'

Mr Drabble leaned back in his chair and laughed. 'Nonsense, lad! You'll enjoy every minute of it, once you arrive. Most of the others wish they were in your shoes, I can tell you. Why, you'll have no trouble getting a scholarship to art college after all this publicity.'

'But I want to be a bargee, sir.'

'A bargee?' Mr Drabble was astounded. He leaned so far out on the back two legs of his chair that he almost came a cropper.

'It's a great life, sir, floating up and down the canal all day . . . .'

'Ah, yes, that would appeal to you, the promise of a nice, lazy time. But I can assure you it's not like that at all. It's extremely hard work, manoeuvring a barge through locks and under tunnels and such. Anyway, your talent lies in quite another direction. You're a born artist, as Mrs Crake tells me she had long suspected.'

'Rotten old liar!' thought Angus. 'Trying to take all the credit.' Aloud, he said: 'You can be your own boss on the canal, sir. There's nobody to bother you once you've loaded your barge up. And if you're interested in birds, sir . . . .'

Birds indeed!

This interview, Mr Drabble decided, was not going at all the way he had planned it. He gave a business-like cough. 'Yes, well, it's time you went back to your classroom, Angus. You'll feel quite differently after next Friday. Believe me, when you've met Sir Desmond Snubbs you won't give barges another thought. Now, I've sorted out all the information you need for the trip, but if your mother has any further problems, tell her to ring me between four and five, any day this week.'

Without quite knowing how it had been managed, Angus found himself standing alone in the corridor with a bundle of official-looking papers under his arm. He began to walk slowly towards his classroom as if in a trance.

Suddenly, a boy called Billy Schofield appeared in front of him.

'Hi, Angus! All fixed up to meet Lord Snotty-nose, are you?'

Angus Lang crackled with rage. He slapped his papers down into a puddle on the nearest window-sill, grabbed Billy Schofield's right ear, dragged him round in a circle and sent him spinning down the corridor. That was more like it! That had shaken off the magic-spell feeling, once and for all.

Chapter 6

'London? What are you talking about?' snapped Mrs Lang. 'If it's a school trip, you know very well we haven't got the money.'

Angus began to explain all over again. His mother evidently hadn't been listening the first time.

'You mean to say you won that prize, then, after all? Well, there must be some mistake. Somebody with the same name or something; there's plenty of Langs about. You can't draw for toffee.'

'Thanks!' said Angus bitterly.

'Well, you can't. You know you can't. I'm only telling the truth. You'd better go and see Mr Drabble in the morning and sort out what's happened.'

'Maybe I can draw. My picture must be some good if they're hanging it in the Taste Gallery.'

'What?' Mrs Lang let go the spoon with which she had been stirring the stew, and Rosco leapt to lick it clean. 'Are you telling me they're going to hang your picture up in a proper art gallery? Next to rude pictures of folks with nothing on? Well, that's disgusting, that is, and you only a child. I don't know what Mr Drabble's thinking of. Give me those papers!'

Mrs Lang snatched at the soggy bundle of documents and spread them out on the kitchen table. She was still reading, with many 'Oooh's and 'Aaaah's and 'Fancy that!'s, when Angus's dad came in.

'Here, look at these! Our Angus has won that prize he was telling us about. Five hundred pounds, it is! Five hundred pounds! He's to go to London to get presented with it. They've even sent train tickets for two.'

'Good for you, then!' grinned Mr Lang to his son. 'I take my hat off to anyone who can earn five hundred quid in one afternoon. I'll go with you to London, if you like.'

'Oh, no you won't! You've your picket line to think of. Anyway, the Headmaster's letter's addressed to me. The presentation's on a Friday. He'd think you'd be working,' Mrs Lang said pointedly. 'Anyway, it's time I had a day out.'

'Suit yourself.' Mr Lang lost interest and started looking round for the evening paper. 'But you'll have to leave our Kevin at your Emily's. I can't be expected to take him with me up the picket.'

'Our Kevin can come with us.'

Angus's heart lurched with alarm. 'There's only two tickets.'

'I'll pay for him myself. Our Emily will lend me a bit until you get your prize money. It's not every day his brother wins a prize, is it, Kevvy? And we can

34

take him to see Buckingham Palace afterwards. He'll like that, won't you, lovey?'

But before he could answer, Kevin, who had been busy sticking his tongue out at Angus behind his mother's back, fell over the dog and began to cry.

'He's not coming! He'll only spoil everything! Look at him now.'

'What a thing to say about your little brother! You oughta be ashamed.'

'He's always in bother. He'll go and fall over or something just at the important bit, and ruin everything.'

Kevin escaped from his mother's embrace to kick Angus on the shin, then ran back and howled louder than ever.

'Oh, hush, love! Mum'll buy you some nice new clothes for London. How about some of them blue velvet pants from Marks's?'

'What about me?' asked Angus.

'You can wear your school uniform. They'll expect it.'

'Oh, great! It's my prize, so he gets new pants. With my money!'

'You needn't worry, son,' Dad butted in. 'There'll be no new pants in this house for a while. As a matter of fact, that five hundred quid's a Godsend, but it's not for wasting. We're going to need every penny of it. This strike looks like lasting till

next December.'

This news sparked off such a terrible outburst from Mrs Lang that Angus slipped from the house and ran and ran until he was out of earshot.

Chapter 7

Thursday, the day before the presentation, was a bustle of preparation. Mrs Lang gave herself a home perm, which was so much of a disaster that she had to go and borrow a floppy hat from her sister Emily. Then she cleaned her shoes for a solid twenty minutes, never heeding that she had used black polish on brown leather. After that, she packed her enormous handbag with such useful items as bandages, throat pastilles, safety pins, kiss-of-life manual, and a novelty scent-bottle shaped like a revolver. You never knew, in a wicked city like London. Mrs Lang had been to London only once before, and that was because she had forgotten to change at Crewe. She remembered it vividly as a place of wild stampedes, stewed tea, bird-droppings, pouring rain and unobliging porters. Yet for the sake of her son's triumph—(and the five hundred pounds)—she was willing to suffer it all again. A great pile of pressed-beef sandwiches was prepared, spread lavishly with mustard to keep out the cold. To these were added two great flasks of coffee, a bag of home-made coconut pyramids and several packets of cheese-and-onion-flavoured potato crisps. All these goodies were to be consumed on the outward journey, despite the fact that Sir

Desmond Snubbs was to entertain them to a five-course luncheon.

'Our Kevin'll be sick before we even get there,' prophesied Angus gloomily. Yet he felt that even this disaster would not shame him as much as his mother's dreadful appearance. Her hair was hideous, her coat was purple and her borrowed hat was a horrible brick-red. Angus knew he would be ashamed of her—and even more ashamed of being ashamed of his own mother. And all that on top of having won the prize by false pretences in the first place!

Angus was sent to bed early with instructions to 'get a good night's sleep', his mother threatening to call him nice and early, so as to have time to examine his ears and fingernails.

'Just you get up right away in the morning, no messing about!'

Angus trailed miserably to his room, wishing only that he might fall asleep at once and, in the fashion of Rip Van Winkle, not wake up again until the whole thing was ancient history. Yet when he did sleep, he wished he hadn't. For then he squirmed and turned in hot and sticky dread, the wild shapes of a nightmare looming round his struggling form. Sir Desmond Snubbs had turned out to be a wicked giant who chased Angus and finally threw him to the sharks in the icy depths of

the river Thames, having first hung Kevin and Mrs Lang round Angus's neck to weight him down. Dawn was actually beginning to seep through the curtains when an exhausted, terrified Angus finally awoke. He lay there trembling for a while, his poor brain in a turmoil ... until inspiration finally struck! Of course! There was one way out of his dilemma; why hadn't he thought of it before? It was so simple, too. Suddenly, Angus smiled.

'He's gone!' yelled Mrs Lang, storming into Angus's room a while later to see why he hadn't responded to her rousing shouts. She rushed hysterically through the house, banging doors and slamming cupboards.

'Where's he gone? We've lost him! He's run off!'

When Mr Lang finally appeared in rumpled pyjamas, he was seized, pushed, dragged and shaken by his wife, who screamed at him to 'Do something, can't you? Don't just stand about. He's supposed to be collecting that five hundred pounds.'

In the end, mostly to shut his wife up, Mr Lang telephoned the police to see if they had news of any accidents or runaway boys. They had not, but once their interest had been aroused they did not intend to leave the matter there. Very soon, a sergeant came round to the house.

Angus's fame had spread. The sergeant knew all about the lad's prize picture, and was sure this was the reason for his disappearance. Could it be nerves, he asked Angus's mother? Nothing of the sort, she retorted. Why, Angus was looking forward to it all; it was his big day; he'd not miss it for a million Munchy bars.

'Yes, but last-minute stage fright . . .' suggested the sergeant.

'Well, all right then, where is he? Where do you go when you've got last-minute stage fright? You find him, then, for we can't!'

At last the sergeant asked if he could take a look round Angus's bedroom.

'He hasn't left a note, if that's what you're thinking.'

'But he might have left a clue.'

Mum, Dad, Kevin and the sergeant trooped upstairs, while Rosco sat howling on the back doorstep as if he knew that Angus was gone forever.

'His bed's been slept in, that's for sure!' cried Mrs Lang, flinging back the door to Angus's room.

'Aye, by a load of Olympic wrestlers,' added Dad, surveying the tortured sheets and blankets.

'H'm!' The sergeant stood for a moment, taking all in but saying nothing. At length he dived down to the bedside rug and tenderly gathered something up. It was a shred of pipe tobacco. Dropping this into one of the plastic bags he always carried, the sergeant turned to the Langs with a confident nod.

'I've never seen you with a pipe, Mr Lang. So either your son's a secret smoker, or he's been kidnapped.'

This made Kevin howl even louder than Rosco, until Mrs Lang took hold of him and shook him.

'Shut up, you big, spoilt baby!' she cried viciously. 'You're always on the moan!'

Chapter 8

At the Taste Gallery, a room had been set aside for the presentation ceremony. There, in a fine gilt frame, in the middle of a white wall, hung the already famous 'Peace' of Angus Lang. Opposite stood a television camera, whose crew were filling in time with a few close-ups of the other pictures. All around them seethed newspaper reporters with their notebooks at the ready, Gallery officials, VIPs and a few plain-clothes policemen. Sir Desmond Snubbs, resplendent in a three-piece, pin-striped suit with red carnation in its buttonhole, glanced edgily at his watch for the umpteenth time. The programme was supposed to be on the air. Could there have been another rail strike? Could the taxi-driver have lost his way? Could young Angus have gone down with the measles at the last minute? Nervously, Sir Desmond's fingers crept to his inside pocket, checking upon the cheque as a best man checks upon the ring. He drew forth an immaculate white handkerchief with which he proceeded to mop his distinguished brow—a gesture watched eagerly by several million viewers. The ceremony was twenty minutes late and the crowd was growing restless. The radio commentator had described the dresses of everyone in sight, including two charwomen who sneaked through the room on their way to their belated elevenses. At last, just when everyone was beginning to suspect the worst, a uniformed policeman appeared. He stood just inside the doorway, looking round. Then he spotted Sir Desmond Snubbs, went over to him and whispered in his ear. Sir Desmond's bushy white eyebrows shot up as he listened with obvious concern. Then he turned and whispered to the official standing next to him. The official whispered to someone else in turn, and gradually the whisper travelled round the room.

'It looks like the boy's been kidnapped!'

The television camera zoomed in on startled faces, the reporters surged, the VIPs twittered on their little gilt chairs like song-birds on golden perches. The plain-clothes policemen sidled furtively about, and the buzzing and twittering grew louder as imaginations practically burst into flames.

'Our live broadcast from the Taste Gallery has been interrupted by some very sensational news,' began the television commentator in a throbbing voice. 'It appears that the young boy prizewinner may have been kidnapped. We shall bring you further details as soon as they are available, but at the moment all we have are rumours. One of the rumours is that after all this sensational publicity, that "Peace" picture may soon be worth a fortune.

Well, as I say, we shall be standing by for further developments, but for the moment we return you to the studio . . . .'

This message bounced from Telstar right into the sitting-room of Cyrus J. Beefenberger, at his villa on Long Island, New York, USA. Cyrus was an art-collector of renown. In fact, at that very moment, without so much as turning his head, he could see two Van Goghs, a Renoir and a couple of Lowrys. Cyrus picked up his ruby-studded telephone.

'Get me my London agent.'

'Yes, Mr Beefenberger.'

'Fast!'

'Right away, Mr Beefenberger.'

'Harry? Is that you? Well now, listen here. You get over to the Taste Gallery right away—(do you hear me, Harry? The Taste Gallery, I said)—and make them an offer for a picture called "Peace", the one painted by some kid or other . . . .'

The line crackled.

'Sure I'm sure! Yeah, I know all about the competition and the kid and everything. It's my job to know every story about every work of art. And it's your job to do as you're told. I don't care how much you have to pay for it; I want that picture. Right?'

'Right, Mr Beefenberger. But—'

'The only butt I know is on one end of a rifle. So

just you go get me that picture, Harry. At the double.'

'Right away, Mr Beefenberger.'

Cyrus slammed down the telephone and turned his head a couple of centimetres to the left. He could now see one Leonardo da Vinci, two large Corots and an Epstein bust. He began to wonder where on earth he was going to hang the 'Peace' when it arrived. Maybe he'd have to throw a Constable away. Problems, problems!

Chapter 9

'It's so peaceful,' said Angus Lang dreamily, 'that I wish I could stay here for ever.'

'Far as I'm concerned you can,' replied Tom the bargee. 'One little 'un like you don't make much difference, and it's nice for me to have a bit of company. 'Specially somebody what appreciates the beauties o' nature. (I do believe I seen a kingfisher just then, back o' them trees.)'

Angus felt flabbergasted at such a carefree approach to life. Tom evidently didn't care tuppence what Angus's mother might think, or how Angus's schooling might suffer. He hadn't even thought about such mundane matters as clean socks, pyjamas or toothbrush, none of which Angus had remembered to bring with him. Angus concluded that none of these things must be really important. Yet he still wore his guilt like a great suit of wrong-size armour.

'My mum will be upset if I don't go home.'

'Do her good. She upset you, didn't she? And tried to spend your money before you'd even laid hands on it. Fair's fair, then. You can send her a postcard when we get to Liverpool.'

It sounded all right, but there was one thing which Tom hadn't thought of. One very important thing—and that was Rosco. Angus was very fond of that dog. He knew that he couldn't live long apart from Rosco, so there was no question of his staying on the barge for ever. On the other hand, he dreaded the thought of going back home whilst his mother was still in a fury. (He could well imagine her face and the sound of her voice when she found he'd disappeared.) So why not compromise? It was Friday. He could spend the weekend with Tom, then go back home on Monday morning, just in time to escape again to school. By then his mother would be so glad to see him—(having thought of him as dead)—that maybe she'd give him a big hug and double his spends. As for that rotten picture, perhaps the fuss would all die down when he didn't turn up for his prize. They could always give it to the runner-up; some girl from the Isle of Man, if he wasn't mistaken. Pity about the loss of the five hundred pounds, but of course it was never really his by rights, and Angus knew he'd never have been able to spend it the way he wanted, in any case. What was left of it.

'Fancy a spot of fishing?' asked Tom. 'There's a rod under that tarpaulin behind you. Let's see how you shape. There's half an hour or so before the next lock. Time to catch us a bite for our dinner.'

Angus was delighted. He'd been fishing with his friends a time or two, but had never possessed a rod

of his own. He took it out from its hiding place and stroked it lovingly. Then he worked out what to do, cast off his line and waited. Life was really beginning to be quite bearable.

Meanwhile, Cyrus J. Beefenberger's London agent, Harry, was rushing up the steps into the Taste Gallery. Here he discovered, in an eminent huddle in one of the offices, Sir Desmond Snubbs himself, and Mr Redford Ragg, the Chairman of the Peace-Among-Nations Inspirational Committee, PANIC.

'I don't really see,' Sir Desmond was saying, 'how I can be blamed for anything that has happened. I am merely giving back the cheque to you because I have been unable to hand it over to the winner.'

'Oh, don't misunderstand me!' cried Redford Ragg, 'Red' to his friends. 'It isn't a question of blame at all. On the contrary! The whole sad affair is—dare I say it?—wonderful publicity for our cause. Of course, we deplore—'

'Excuse me!' Harry interrupted. 'I'm looking for the Chairman of PANIC. Do you know if he's still in the building?'

'You're looking right at him,' Redford smiled. But Sir Desmond cut in coldly, 'No more reporters! We've had quite enough publicity for one day. Out you go, young man, and please close the door

behind you.'

Harry was not accustomed to being taken for a reporter. He felt offended, tried to express his indignation and was forcibly seized by Sir Desmond before he could explain. Sir Desmond was at the end of his tether. He felt he had been made to look foolish in public, and now he was being hounded by the press. His privacy was being invaded. He shook poor Harry so fiercely that Harry's new dental plate slipped out of position. Perhaps it was this which made him less articulate than usual, for when he did finally make himself heard, the other two could only chorus: 'WHAT DID YOU SAY?'

'I said,' repeated Harry, clicking his denture back into place, 'that my American client wishes to make an offer of 50,000 dollars for the "Peace" picture.'

Sir Desmond was astounded; Redford gaped, then repeated the figure in utter disbelief.

'All right then, a hundred thousand,' Harry urged.

'But you can't possibly . . . .'

'Two hundred thousand.'

'You seem to be under the mistaken impression . . . .'

'Five hundred thousand!'

'My dear chap, this is ridiculous!' Sir Desmond cried, mopping his brow, in his confusion, with a green felt pen-wiper from the desk behind him.

'All right then, one million dollars. How about that?'

Sir Desmond turned crimson; Redford Ragg turned greenish-grey. 'I don't believe it!' Redford croaked.

'Two million dollars!'

'No, don't say another word! You're breaking my heart. You see, the picture isn't mine to sell. It would have been if the lad had come forward and claimed his prize. He would have had the five hundred pounds, and we, in return, would have had the picture to use as we wanted. But he didn't turn up, so it still belongs to him.' Here Redford wobbled and had to sit down.

'We must find him, then, mustn't we?' cried Harry, already fearing the wrath of his American client. 'One little lad can't have got far away, all on his own.'

'He's probably been kidnapped,' Sir Desmond announced. 'In fact, the more I hear of this whole incredible episode, the more certain I am that he has been kidnapped. There's a great deal more to this than meets the eye.'

Chapter 10

By Saturday morning, Angus had learned a great deal about fishing. He had actually caught one or two small fish, but that was not really what mattered. The game was the thing.

"Course, there's nothing very big in this canal,' said Tom consolingly. But for once Tom was wrong. Not half an hour later, just as they were coming within sight of Waxford Lock, Angus felt a mighty pull on his line. Eyes gleaming triumphantly, he began to draw the fish in. He thought he had never felt so happy in the whole of his life.

The fish turned out to be a pike, and was a great deal stronger than Angus had imagined. There was a jerk, followed immediately by a stronger jerk, and suddenly, with a startled cry, Angus found himself diving head-first into the chilly black water, having left one of his shoes behind. The rod flew through the air and the pike escaped, dragging the rod down-water after him.

'Tom! Help! I'm drow . . . glug, glug!'

Tom was by this time on the far side of the barge, concentrating on the lock ahead, and on two idiots in a pleasure boat who were sailing far too fast towards him. In any case, though he would never admit it, Tom was more than a little deaf. The barge moved purposefully on, leaving Angus floundering wildly in the water.

The pleasure boat, now bearing down on Angus, was called *Molly*. A soppy name for a boat, as Simon Crickle had remarked to his friend Ferdie Flapp when they had first looked the vessel over.

'If you want to call it Goliath, or Jaws, or Pterodactyl, feel free,' Ferdie had replied, heaving his great, framed rucksack on board. 'Just so long as we get a nice, uneventful holiday.'

Simon and Ferdie were students fresh from examinations and more than ready for a spell of relaxation before the dreaded results. Yet 'uneventful' was to be the least appropriate word for their trip. Why, that very morning, not only had they stunned a duck, stalled the engine, almost capsized in Waxford Lock and been abused by some loud-mouthed bargee, but they had now spotted a body in the water.

'Man overboard!' yelled Ferdie, rushing for the boat-hook. He could be a man of action in a crisis, though he regarded himself primarily as a poet. (So far on this trip he had sat for hours with a notebook open on his lap, gazing at water, banks or sky with a bemused expression and occasionally sighing very deeply. Though after three days it must be admitted that his notebook was still open at page one.)

Simon flung down his guitar and rushed to

help ... taking care however, to fling the instrument safely on to a pile of sacks. That guitar meant more to Simon than a plague to an undertaker. If Simon didn't manage a degree, then he would shoot to fame as a pop-star overnight. (In fact, there were times when Simon actually hoped and prayed that he would fail all his examinations.) Now, however, all thoughts of fame laid by, he dived into the water. Shuddering with shock in the painful cold, he struck out towards the dark shape snatching desperately at their wake.

Simon grabbed Angus and Ferdie grabbed Simon. Soon, they had hauled on board a wet, heavy, gasping, terrified young boy.

Although there was no need for anything as drastic as the kiss of life, the boy did look a sorry mess. His face was blotched, his hair was weedy and his clothes were sopping rags. What's more, a great big lump was rising where he must have caught the back of his head on something sharp. As a final indignity, he had only one shoe.

However, by the time this waif had been rolled up in a warm, dry towel and given a mug of hot cocoa, he began to look a little better.

'What's your name, son?'

'Er—' Angus eyed his captors furtively. 'I—I can't remember.'

'Were you on a boat?'

'Don't know.'

'Can't you remember anything?'

'Nope. Just feel this lump on the back of my head,' said Angus with more confidence.

Angus was put to bed in the spare bunk, then Simon and Ferdie withdrew to discuss what to do with him.

'Do you think he has lost his memory?'

'Could have, with a bump like that. But it's more likely he's up to something, and doesn't want us to find out.'

'What would you have been up to at that age? Running away from home?'

'Too true, if I'd had half a chance. Always kept my savings and a bar of chocolate ready, but somehow it never came off.'

'I managed it once,' mused Simon. 'Then some nosy old biddy saw me pinching the birds' crusts in the park, and handed me over to the police. They scared me half to death, they did.'

'Yeah, we won't do that to him. If we handle it right, we can persuade him to go home of his own free will.'

'You think?'

'Let's find out who he is first. One of us stay with the lad, the other go ashore for a local newspaper. If he's from round here, it'll say he's missing.'

'Better still, we could try the local pubs, ask a few

questions there.'

'What a good idea!' Ferdie beamed. 'I'll be off, then, right away.'

Chapter 11

'I tell you I saw young Angus at six o'clock yesterday morning,' the milkman said. 'He was running off across the fields towards the canal.'

'Well, why didn't you say so before?'

'Nobody asked me, that's why. I've been busy. I didn't even know the lad was missing.'

The police sergeant, who had been questioning the villagers for hours, felt at last that his patience had been rewarded. 'Nobody with him?'

'Not a soul about. Never is, at that time in the morning. Lovely and peaceful, as a rule.'

'Looks as though he might have fallen in the canal and drowned, then.'

'Well, for pity's sake don't go telling his mother that. She'll have a fit.'

'She'll soon find out why we're dragging the canal.'

'He can't swim either, young Angus can't.'

'Oh, dear! There's a tragedy for somebody every day . . . .'

'Here, just a minute!' interrupted the milkman's wife. 'I wonder if he was the lad I saw the other day, on Tom Heston's barge? Having the time of his life, he was, running up and down with bits of rope, and a face as black as coal.'

'Old Tom Heston wouldn't kidnap anybody. He's as mild and gentle as a baby's bath-suds.'

'Nobody said he'd kidnapped the lad. But he might have given him a ride.'

'H'm. I suppose it's worth a try,' said the sergeant, scribbling in his notebook. 'I could find out whether Tom's passed here today, and if he has, we'll have him followed up the canal and search his barge.'

They did. A police car drew up near Waxford Lock, just as Tom's barge had gone through.

"Morning, Mr Heston. Got a young helper with you today, I believe?'

'Maybe I have, maybe I haven't,' Tom said warily. If the police were asking questions, it looked as though young Angus was in some sort of trouble. Tom was certainly not going to be the one to betray him. He glanced cautiously about him. Angus was nowhere to be seen. The lad must have spotted the police car coming, and hidden himself somewhere.

'Mind if we take a look round, then?' One policeman was already leaping on board, and another looked ready to follow him.

'Yes, I do mind! I've got a load here has to be in Liverpool tomorrow. Can't hang about talking to you lot.'

'That's all right. Just carry on, Mr Heston, and we'll come with you. We'll get the car to pick us up further on.'

'What's up, then?' asked Tom cautiously.

'Lad missing. Thought he might have stowed away on board. You never know.'

'I know!' cried Tom indignantly. 'I know every inch of this barge. There's no lad stowed away on here.' By now, Tom had had a chance to cast his eye over the barge pretty thoroughly, and he could see that Angus was not there. The boy had very likely slipped quietly into the water to dodge his pursuers. Tom did not know that Angus could not swim, and he decided the best way he could help his young friend was to put as much distance between him and the police as possible.

'Look round if you like,' Tom grudgingly invited, as he furtively began to increase the barge's speed.

On the table in the little cabin was a dark brown leather pouch. The first policeman picked it up and sniffed it. Then he signalled to his companion. They opened the pouch, took out a pinch of tobacco which they dropped carefully into a plastic bag, then continued their search. Finally, half-hidden under a huge tarpaulin, they found a shoe. A boy's shoe with—(as school regulations insisted)—a name written carefully inside. The name was Angus Lang.

'If you'll just pull into the side as soon as convenient . . .' one policeman said to Tom.

'. . . We'll get somebody over right away to take

your load on to Liverpool,' finished the other.

Tom, normally so calm, grew quite alarmed. 'What's going on? Here, what are you doing with them handcuffs? What are you playing at? I ain't done nothing wrong.'

'We'll see about that at the station,' said the first policeman grimly.

Chapter 12

'"MILLIONAIRE" ANGUS STILL MISSING' shrieked the Saturday morning headlines. Even *The Times* and the *Guardian* ran the story as their lead. All had photographs of Angus, plucked eagerly from the family album by Mrs Lang, who vowed she would do anything to find her son, millionaire or not. She cried a lot as she told the reporters: 'His dad's out on strike, an' all. And you should see his little brother Kevin! He's that upset! And the dog's fretting something awful.'

'Of course,' commented Angus's dad with practical good sense, 'the lad's only a minor. If he doesn't turn up, then that picture belongs to me.'

What with the police, the newspapers, the television, the messages of sympathy and the nosy neighbours, Mrs Lang hadn't had such an exciting time for years. It was almost better than the trip to London would have been. Not that she wasn't grieving. Anyone who has come so close to a million pounds and not been able to lay hands on it will know exactly how she felt. As for Kevin, he was coming down with chicken pox, only nobody had time to notice.

The sensation of Angus Lang's disappearance looked like lasting for days, or even weeks. It seemed that only a major disaster, such as Star Wars really breaking out, could oust it from the headlines. Yet by Saturday lunchtime an even greater sensation had burst upon the news-hungry world. The 'Peace' picture had been stolen!

It seemed that just before Gallery opening time on Saturday morning, the night-watchman was found unconscious in a dark corner of the Taste Gallery with his key-bunch missing. There was an ominously bare patch on the wall where 'Peace' had hung, yet the alarm had never sounded. It had been expertly dismantled.

'Top grade professionals!' cried Sir Desmond Snubbs when he heard the news. 'Those villains knew exactly what they were looking for, and when and how to get it. That picture must be worth even more that we thought.'

'You can't help admiring their cheek,' said Redford Ragg ruefully.

The art world was rocked like an empty canoe going over Niagara Falls. There had been nothing like this since the Mona Lisa was attacked. Cables and telex messages flew back and forth like midges in a swamp, and all the ports and airports were alerted for the thieves. Had they grabbed not only the picture but its artist, too? Did they intend to keep young Angus prisoner, forcibly painting more and more pictures for them to sell? The whole thing

had become an International Incident. Questions were to be asked at the United Nations General Assembly as to whether the greed of the rich should be allowed to force up prices high enough to put children's lives at risk.

'The more famous and valuable that painting becomes, the less chance we have of finding that boy alive,' said a spokesman from the Save the Children fund.

Meanwhile, the battered night-watchman regained consciousness and started mumbling something about loose false teeth.

'You haven't got them in, love,' a kindly nurse assured him. 'Look, here they are, in this jar on top of your locker.'

Chapter 13

'Look, we know who you are,' said Simon Crickle kindly. 'Ferdie here has just been ashore to do a bit of research. It seems there's a great hue and cry on, and we think we'd better take you home.'

'No!' cried Angus in alarm.

'You haven't really lost your memory,' Ferdie grinned. 'I tried that once, at about your age, when I broke a jeweller's window with my football. But it's ever so easy to detect. You can't get away with it for more than an hour.'

'I have lost my memory,' Angus insisted. 'I've no idea how I came to be on this canal.'

'Oh, you do know it's a canal, then, and not some river?'

'Well, I'm guessing, aren't I?' Angus's cheeks turned pink.

'And I'm guessing your folks will be ever so glad to have you back.'

'No, they won't! They only want the money.'

Simon grinned. 'What money's that, then?'

Angus knew that he had given himself away, and the best thing to do seemed to be to burst into tears.

'Hey, cheer up! I've brought some fish and chips back with me.' Ferdie began unwrapping a great, greasy parcel, the smell of which was very tempting

to a hungry, growing lad. Before he knew it, Angus
had wiped his eyes on his blanket and started
tucking in.

'We'll come with you and explain,' said Simon
when the tale was told at last. 'We'll say you were so
nervous of the presentation that you decided you
daren't go through with it. After all, that's most of
the truth.'

'My mum will kill me!'

'No, she won't. If you could see her now . . . .'

Eventually, the two students managed to persuade young Angus that they were right. After all,
what else could he do? He couldn't stay with them
for ever, and anyway, Ferdie had also brought back
news of Tom's arrest. It was up to Angus to sort that
out as soon as possible.

'All right; you win,' he told them without enthu-
siasm.

Angus had to borrow a pair of Ferdie's old track-
shoes, since he had only one shoe of his own. The
track-shoes were a couple of sizes too big, but when
stuffed with newspapers they didn't seem too bad.
Angus found he could shuffle along quite well.
Then he put on some borrowed clothes and they set
off. The three of them walked along the towpath
until they came to a stile. This led into a field, which
led to another field, which finally led to a road. By
the roadside was a bus stop, and there they waited

for twenty minutes, until finally a lorry came along.

'You lot want a lift, then? Where you going?'

'Bordham,' said Ferdie. 'Only a little place. Do you know where it is?'

'Bordham? 'Course I do! It's the one with the nasty bend in the High Street. My pal's wheel come off there the other week, and he went slap through the Post Office window. Could've been nasty.'

With some misgivings, the trio clambered aboard, but they did not have long to worry. Almost immediately the driver diverted their thoughts with an exciting tale.

'Ain't half been some goings-on at Speke airport this morning, I can tell you. That's where I've just come from, Speke airport. Held me up for two hours, they did. Police swarming all over the place, looking for some art robbers or something.'

Angus's ears pricked up.

'Did they catch them?'

'I'll say they did! What a hullaballoo! Seems these robbers had chased up from London, thinking the London airports would more likely be watched, but the police come and stopped this plane, just when it was taxi-ing off to America. I saw 'em drag this bloke down the steps and off that plane like he was a sack of turnips late for a royal banquet. Dragged him so bloomin' rough his false teeth fell out.'

'What about the picture?' asked Angus breathlessly.

'Still had it under his arm in a canvas bag. But that wasn't all, not half! This bloke was supposed to have kidnapped some kid or other, as well. They searched the plane, searched all the airport, toilets, waiting-rooms, store-rooms, vehicles, my lorry ... thought I'd be there till next Christmas.'

'Quite a carry-on!' remarked Ferdie, winking at Simon. 'I'm glad we're not mixed up in it.'

Angus groaned. 'How long will it take us to get back to Bordham?' He looked so impatient all of a

sudden that you'd have thought he had an ice-cream sundae waiting there, melting away before he could get a spoon to it.

Chapter 14

Mrs Lang threw her arms around her son and almost squashed him flat. As for Rosco, he leaped and barked and nearly went berserk.

'Oh, Angus! My lamb! My baby! My treasure!' cried Mrs Lang with exaggerated passion, yet spilling quite genuine tears.

'Hello, Mum!' Angus muttered anxiously, trying to wriggle free to give Rosco a cuddle. It was only a matter of time, he felt, before his mother's mood changed back to normal. Meantime, he had to admit it was quite nice to have a fuss made over him.

At length, Mrs Lang dried her eyes and stood back to admire her offspring. It was then she noticed the strange assortment of garments in which Angus was dressed. A too-big sweater of Ferdie's; Simon's oldest jeans, rolled up at the bottoms and taken in at the waist with safety-pins; and the track-shoes stuffed with paper.

'Grief and sorrow! You look like a walking jumble-sale! What's happened to your good school uniform?'

'It's all right, Mrs Lang.' Simon produced a large parcel in a damp plastic bag. 'His own clothes are here. They got a bit wet, so we lent him some of

ours, not wanting him to catch cold. If you hang them up in the kitchen they'll soon dry off.'

'Wet?' Mrs Lang put a wealth of meaning into that one word. 'But it hasn't rained all week.'

'Here we go!' thought Angus resignedly. Things were promising to slip back to normal even more quickly than he'd imagined. He went and buried his head in Rosco's shaggy coat.

But Mrs Lang knew her manners. Further questions must wait. These two young men, however scruffy they might look, had brought her son back to her, and they must be given a cup of tea. She bustled about, setting a tray with the best cups and saucers, and even producing a plate of coconut pyramids, left over from the cancelled trip. And all the time she chattered on, mostly of how upset she'd been, and what a sensation it had all caused, and the way she'd searched, and wept, and broken her heart, and vowed she'd do anything to get Angus back.

'I suppose you know your picture got stolen? And some poor old night-watchman got bumped on the head as well? Anyway, you needn't worry, son, the policeman just came to tell me they've got it back. He'd just had a phone call from Liverpool, it seems. They stopped some villain at the airport, trying to fly off to America with your picture, if you please!' She turned to Simon and Ferdie. 'It's a lovely picture, you know. He's quite an artist, our Angus.'

'Did they have it with them, Mum? Did they give it you?'

'What, the picture? Oh no, not yet. It's still in Liverpool, and it has to be gone over for fingerprints and the like. Policeman said it would be a week or two before they handed it back. And I want to talk to you about that.'

'I've got to go and see the police, Mum. Right away. I've got stuff to tell them.' Angus, keen to change the subject, had guessed what his mother was going to say.

'It can wait five minutes, surely. You've not even said hello to our Kevin yet, and him in bed with chicken pox. Now, about that picture. I want you to take it out of the competition.'

'Eh?' said Angus rudely.

'You know why! You knew the rules as well as I did, right from the start.' But in case he had forgotten, she picked up a sheet of paper and started reading from it. 'Any prizewinning picture will belong to PANIC, to use as they please for the promotion of their cause.'

'Yes, well, that's okay by me,' said Angus. 'It always was.'

Mrs Lang cast her eyes up to Heaven. 'This lad wants his head seeing to,' she told the others. 'If his picture stays in the competition, he wins five hun-

dred pounds, and that's all. If he withdraws it, and sells it himself, he could be a millionaire. Did you hear what that American chap was offering—?'

'Five hundred pounds will do me nicely,' said Angus stoutly. 'I'd rather PANIC had the million. It's time somebody did something for a bit of peace.'

The fairy tale feeling crept over him again, though this time it was more of a Jack-the-Giant-Killer sensation. Angus had power at last, and he was going to use it properly.

'PANIC could do a lot of good with that money, Mrs Lang,' agreed Simon.

'They'd waste it. Anway, even if they didn't waste

it, what good is one little million pounds to set the whole world to rights?'

'It's a start, that's what,' said Ferdie. 'You've got to start somewhere. And think of the publicity, all for peace!'

Mrs Lang regarded the two students suspiciously. 'I do believe you two belong to that crazy lot yourselves. Well, you're not going to make us change our minds.'

'My mind's made up,' declared Angus even more stoutly. 'And it is my picture. Money's not everything,' he added, astonished to find that he believed it.

'I never heard such selfish cheek in all my life! Here we are, up to our necks in mortgages and hire-purchases, and our Kevin wanting a new trike and I don't know what, and your dad out on strike . . . .'

Just then the front door flew open and in marched Mr Lang, bristling with indignation.

'Sold down the river!' he shouted before he had even spotted his son. 'Strike's over. We're going back on Monday.'

'Hi, Dad! What does "sold down the river" mean?' asked Angus, rushing to meet his father.

'It means they've come to their senses at last,' said Mrs Lang with satisfaction. 'Just as you will when you've drunk that cup of tea and thought properly about what I've said.'

Chapter 15

The next sensation was that the art thief who had been captured on the plane escaped from custody on his way to jail. What's more, despite a thorough search, the man was never found, although of course the police still had the picture safe and sound.

It was almost a month before the picture was returned to the Taste Gallery, so that the presentation ceremony could be organised afresh. Nothing would shake Angus Lang's resolve to leave his picture in the competition, and he had even made up his mind that this time he would really go along to the presentation and get it over with. That seemed the only way to ensure that PANIC would have its chance to sell the picture and grow rich. To Angus's surprise, his dad supported him.

'We're not cut out to be millionaires,' he said after a deal of thought. 'You read of folks who've won the pools, and then had a right old miserable time of it—thousands of begging letters, and sponging friends, and too much drinking and gambling and carrying on. Let's just be thankful we've got our lad back, and done our bit for a better future.'

Two against one. Mrs Lang had to give in, though she intended to say 'I told you so!' for the rest of her life, whenever they happened to be short of money. On the other hand, she suddenly found she was proud of her son's unselfishness, which she began to stretch to include herself. 'We're doing it for the best for everybody,' she told the neighbours grandly. 'There's many a one would have snatched at all they could get, but not this family! We'll manage quite well by our own efforts, thank you very much!'

As the Presentation Day came round again, there was much the same bustle of preparation. This time, though, as Mr Lang was now earning again, and as the occasion looked like being a hundred times more newsworthy, Mrs Lang invested in a biscuit-coloured two-piece outfit with matching straw hat, which really looked quite smart. What's more, she had her hair done properly at the hair-dresser's.

In the end, five of them travelled to London together, Mr Lang having been granted a special day off work, and Tom the bargee having also been invited along, at Angus's insistence and expense. It seemed the least he could to to make up for the indignity that Tom had suffered that Saturday morning.

Not only did the little party take a taxi, with no thought of cost, but young Kevin wasn't sick at all, in spite of having eaten two sausage rolls, a cream bun and a monster bag of Chipples on the train.

Sir Desmond Snubbs was a trifle edgy, remembering the previous occasion and the violent events that had followed. But he looked every bit as smart, this time with a red rose in his buttonhole, and his speech was even better rehearsed than before. For this time there were even two Lords and a Royal in the audience, and the news had just come through that the 'Peace' picture was to be used as a postage-stamp illustration. If only that boy turned up!

Angus did turn up, ten minutes early, and was immediately pinned into a corner by a make-up lady who proceeded to comb his hair in a different direction, and dab at his face with a great, tickly powder-puff. Then his jacket was given a brush, his tie was straightened, his shirt-collar smoothed, his socks pulled up, until he began to look quite human. At last he was led forth, to stand on a special little dais in front of his picture, face to face with the great Sir Desmond Snubbs.

It was a stomach-churning moment. There was the television camera, moving steadily, relentlessly, towards him. There was the radio commentator prattling away quietly into his microphone. There were the crowds, the VIPs sitting on their little gilt chairs, the newspaper reporters and their cameramen, the private detectives clustered round the Royal, art critics, posh onlookers and his mum,

dad, Kevin and Tom. Tom winked, but Angus wasn't looking. He had fixed his eyes firmly on his feet. A hush descended. Sir Desmond cleared his throat.

'Your Royal Highness, my Lords, Ladies and Gentlemen....' The presentation had begun!

As Sir Desmond took off into his speech, which was by no means short, Angus plucked up the courage to lift his eyes and stare around him. He soon wished he hadn't, for the sight of all those well-dressed people and those popping flash-blubs and those earphoned, shirt-sleeved cameramen, was enough to terrify a tiger. He turned his eyes away again and glanced instead at the wall behind him, where his picture had pride of place. It stood out a few inches from the wall, because behind it a special alarm had been installed. Angus could see well-disguised wires running hither and thither, and could not help feeling proud that people had gone to all this trouble over his little work of art.

And then he froze. He had spotted something else; something very strange indeed, which was nothing to do with the wires or the security or even the presentation ceremony. It was the picture of 'Peace' itself. There was something wrong with it!

Suddenly, in the middle of one of Sir Desmond's nicely rounded sentences, Angus yelled: 'Hey, that's not my picture! There should be a big black blob on the end of the nose. It's a fake, a copy, a forgery!'

Far away, in a villa on Long Island, Cyrus J. Beefenberger, who was watching the programme live, began to chuckle. Propped against his arm-chair was a Constable in a massive gold frame, which he had had to take down to make room for his latest acquisition.

'Peace, perfect peace!' he sighed contentedly.

Unlike Mr Lang, who was remarking at that very

moment to an excited newspaper reporter: 'There'll be no peace now until she's started World War Three over that dratted picture!'

Other great reads from **Red Fox**

Discover the hilarious world of Red Fox younger fiction!

ALIENS FOR BREAKFAST   Jonathan Etra and Stephanie Spinner

Richard's new cereal is *really* exciting – it contains Aric who has been beamed down from another planet to save the Earth from alien invasion.

ISBN 0 09 981550 8   £2.25

BILLY AND THE GHASTLY GHOST   Mick Gowar

Billy is convinced he has seen a ghost in the graveyard – but proving it to the rest of his class is difficult.

ISBN 0 09 981490 0   £2.99

BILLY AND THE MAN-EATING PLANT
Mick Gower

Billy has to come up with a prizewinning project for the class prize – but he never seems to have the time.

ISBN 0 09 981500 1   £2.50

THANKS FOR THE SARDINE   Laura Beaumont

Aggie decides that her boring Aunts need reforming so she arranges for them to have some training.

ISBN 0 09 997900 4   £2.99

MERVYN'S REVENGE   Leone Peguero

Mervyn the cat is outraged when his family go away without him, and he plots revenge with feline cunning.

ISBN 0 09 997520 3   £2.50

Have some supernatural fun with Jonathan's ghost

Dave is just an ordinary schoolboy – except he happens to be a ghost, and only his friend, Jonathan, can see him. With his love of mischief, Dave creates quite a bit of trouble for Jonathan to explain away – but he can also be an extremely useful friend to have when Jonathan's in a fix.

JONATHAN'S GHOST

Jonathan's starting at a new school – but who needs humans when you've got a ghost for a friend?

ISBN 0 09 968850 6   £2.50

SPITFIRE SUMMER

An old wartime ghost seems to be haunting Jonathan – and only Dave can help him.

ISBN 0 09 968850 6   £2.50

THE SCHOOL SPIRIT

A trip to an old mansion brings Jonathan into contact with a triangle of evil determined to find a new victim.

ISBN 0 09 974620 4   £2.50

JONATHAN AND THE SUPERSTAR

Everyone at Jonathan's school thinks Jason Smythe is wonderful – except Dave. Dave senses trouble afoot . . .

ISBN 0 09 995120 7   £2.50

Other great reads from **Red Fox**

Discover the wacky world of Spacedog and Roy by Natalie Standiford

Spacedog isn't really a dog at all – he's an alien lifeform from the planet Queekrg, who just happens to *look* like a dog. It's a handy form of disguise – but he's not sure he'll *ever* get used to the food!

SPACEDOG AND ROY

Roy is quite surprised to find an alien spacecraft in his garden – but that's nothing to the surprise he gets when Spacedog climbs out.

ISBN 0 09 983650 5   £2.99

SPACEDOG AND THE PET SHOW

Life becomes unbearable for Spacedog when he's entered for the local pet show and a French poodle falls in love with him.

ISBN 0 09 983660 2   £2.99

SPACEDOG IN TROUBLE

When Spacedog is mistaken for a stray and locked up in the animal santuary, he knows he's in big trouble.

ISBN 0 09 983670 X   £2.99

SPACEDOG THE HERO

When Roy's father goes away he makes Spacedog the family watchdog – but Spacedog is scared of the dark. What can he do?

ISBN 0 09 983680 7   £2.99

Other great reads from **Red Fox**

Have a bundle of fun with the wonderful Pat Hutchins

Pat Hutchins' stories are full of wild adventure and packed with outrageous humour for younger readers to enjoy.

FOLLOW THAT BUS

A school party visit to a farm ends in chaotic comedy when two robbers steal the school bus.

ISBN 0 09 993220 2   £2.99

THE HOUSE THAT SAILED AWAY

An hilarious story of a family afloat, in their house, in the Pacific Ocean. No matter what adventures arrive, Gran always has a way to deal with them.

ISBN 0 09 993200 8   £2.99

RATS!

Sam's ploys to persuade his parents to let him have a pet rat eventually meet with success, and with Nibbles in the house, life is never the same again.

ISBN 0 09 993190 7   £2.50

Other great reads from **Red Fox**

Enjoy Jean Ure's stories of school and home life.

JO IN THE MIDDLE

The first of the popular Peter High series. When Jo starts at her new school, she determines never again to be plain, ordinary Jo-in-the-middle.

ISBN 0 09 997730 3   £2.99

FAT LOLLIPOP

The second in the Peter High series. When Jo is invited to join the Laing Gang, she's thrilled – but she also feels guilty because it means she's taking Fat Lollipop's place.

ISBN 0 09 997740 0   £2.99

A BOTTLED CHERRY ANGEL

A story of everyday school life – and the secrets that lurk beneath the surface.

ISBN 0 09 951370 6   £1.99

FRANKIE'S DAD

Frankie can't believe it when her mum marries horrible Billie Small and she has to go and live with him and his weedy son, Jasper. If only her real dad would come and rescue her . . .

ISBN 0 09 959720 9   £1.99

YOU TWO

A classroom story about being best friends – and the troubles it can bring before you find the right friend.

ISBN 0 09 938310 1   £1.95

Other great reads from **Red Fox**

Giggle and groan with a Red Fox humour book!

Nutty, naughty and quite quite mad, the Red Fox humour list has a range of the silliest titles you're likely to see on a bookshelf! Check out some of our weird and wonderful books and we promise you'll have a ribticklingly good read!

MIAOW! THE CAT JOKE BOOK – Susan Abbott

Be a cool cat and paws here for the purrfect joke! Get your claws into this collection of howlers all about our furry friends that will have you feline like a grinning Cheshire Cat!

ISBN 0 09 998460 1 £1.99

THE SMELLY SOCKS JOKE BOOK – Susan Abbott

Hold your nose . . . here comes the funniest and foulest joke book you're likely to read for a while! Packed with pungent puns and reeking with revolting riddles, this one is guaranteed to leave you gasping for air!

ISBN 0 09 956270 7 £1.99

TUTANKHAMUN IS A BIT OF A MUMMY'S BOY
– Michael Coleman

Have you ever dreaded taking home your school report or a letter from the Head? You're in good company! Did you know that Shakespeare was really "hopeless at English" and that Christopher Columbus had "absolutely no sense of direction"? There's fifty other previously unpublished school reports which reveal hilarious secrets about the famous which not many people know . . .

ISBN 0 09 988180 2 £2.99

THE FISH AND CHIPS JOKE BOOK – Ian Rylett

This book comes complete with a fish-and-chips scratch and sniff panel so you can sniff while you snigger at this delicious collection of piping-hot pottiness! Your tastebuds will be tickled no end with this mouth-watering concoction of tasty gags so tuck into a copy today! It's a feast of fun!

ISBN 0 09 995040 5 £2.99

Join the RED FOX Reader's Club

The Red Fox Readers' Club is for readers of all ages. All you have to do is ask your local bookseller or librarian for a Red Fox Reader's Club card. As an official Red Fox Reader you will qualify for your own Red Fox Reader's Clubpack – full of exciting surprises! If you have any difficulty obtaining a Red Fox Readers' Club card please write to: Random House Children's Books Marketing Department, 20 Vauxhall Bridge Road, London SW1V 2SA.